Spirit Storm

Also by E.J. Stevens

Spirit Guide

She Smells the Dead
Spirit Guide
Legend of Witchtrot Road (Coming 2011)

Dark Poetry Collections

From the Shadows
Shadows of Myth and Legend

Spirit Storm

Spirit Guide Series Book Two

E.J. Stevens

Sacred Oaks Press

Published by Sacred Oaks Press
Sacred Oaks, 221 Sacred Oaks Lane, Wells, Maine 04090

First Printing (trade paperback edition), December 2010

Stevens, E.J.
Spirit Storm / E.J. Stevens

ISBN 978-0-9842475-3-0 (trade pbk.)

Printed in the United States of America

PUBLISHER'S NOTE
This is a work of fiction. Names, characters, places, and incidents either are the product of the author's imagination or are used fictitiously, and any resemblance to actual persons, living or dead, business establishments, events, or locales is entirely coincidental.

Chapter 1

October 30th Salem, Massachusetts

"*A* Pox Upon All Thieves," read the sign hanging at eye level on the wall behind the glass case. I stifled a shudder and tried to distract myself from the task at hand. I was about to attempt grand theft amulet from an occult shop known to be run by witches. *Son of a dung beetle. How did I get myself into this mess?*

The words were painted in an old-fashioned font and the sign was covered in a false patina of age. My mind latched onto an old memory of my grandmother teaching me the tricks of tole painting. I remember her patiently demonstrating the technique of speckling, layering, and then using tea for the finishing touch.

"See it's nothing," my mind screamed desperately. "It's not even old." Old or not, the sign still filled me with dread.

I was grasping for anything which might distract me, but thoughts of my grandmother only deepened my sense of guilt. I may be rebellious, but I wasn't the kind of girl to steal from anyone. Except now. I felt like I was on a slippery slope to Hell. *Good thing I wore my boots.*

Chapter 2

October 20th Maine

I shivered as Calvin ran his hand down my cheek and not from the cool autumn breeze swirling leaves around the school parking lot. I pressed myself against him, a little voice in the back of my head only slightly concerned I might impale him on one of the many safety pins covering my shirt. He tilted my head back and leaned in to kiss me. *I am so in love with you Calvin Miller.*

As our lips touched I felt a vibrating against my hip that didn't have anything to do with love or raging hormones.

"Sorry," Cal mumbled against my lips as he reached for his phone. The sleeve of his frayed sweater caught on one of my safety pins and his phone went flying onto the pavement.

"I guess I'm the one that's sorry," I said trying to extract his sweater from my shirt.

"I meant to ask earlier," he said, raising an eyebrow. "Is there a reason why you're wearing about ten pounds of safety pins today?"

I laughed, still attempting to unhook the threads of his sweater. I was tempted to grab clippers from my backpack, but was trying to lessen the damage. Not that I minded being attached to Cal. *Not at all.*

"Emma and I were doing more research and some people believe iron and steel help to repel spirits," I answered.

"I thought that was just for fairies," he said.

3

"Well, it depends on the source," I said. "Some of the books and Internet sites claim that iron and steel also hurts the dead. Other sources even claim fairies actually are spirits. Hence, my crazy awesome safety pin shirt."

"So it's kind of like chain mail for spirits," he said.

"Exactly," I said, finally pulling the last strand of yarn from the offending pin. "There, you're free wolf boy."

Calvin reached down for his phone, but froze part way. His phone was open and the picture which had been sent to him was on the screen. My brain was having trouble processing what I was looking at. There was fur, and limbs, and...oh God, there was the glassy eye of a dead wolf. I looked up at Cal's face and could tell the wolf must have been one of the members of his pack. Something bad had happened. *Something very, very bad.*

Cal's phone suddenly started vibrating, making it dance epileptically along the pavement, and we both nearly jumped out of our skins. *Oh why did my mind have to conjure up* that *image?*

With a shudder, Calvin reached down and grabbed the phone. Pressing the button to answer he closed his eyes and brought the phone to his ear. "Simon?" Cal asked.

"Right on one," Simon quipped, though his tone quickly turned serious. "We have a problem. Did you get the photo I sent you?"

"Yeah, it just came through," Cal said. "Is...is it what it looks like?"

"If it looks like a dead wolf, then yes, it's what it looks like," Simon answered.

I watched Cal's Adam's apple rise and fall with his swallowing. He was obviously trying to keep it together and avoid being sick. I really hoped he managed to control the gorge rising in his throat. Some people are social yawners, but I have the unpleasant habit of social yacking. If Cal puked, I was so totally going to start uncontrollably puking on his shoes. Hurling on my boyfriend would definitely not help this situation. *You better not throw up Calvin Miller.*

4

"Do we know who it is?" Cal asked. He didn't ask if the wolf was one of the Old Blood. *He already knew.*

"Looks like he was an accountant named Gavin Sanders," Simon replied. "He worked in the city and would come out here to the woods on his way home at the end of the work week and go for a run in wolf form. His way to unwind, I guess. I found a pile of his clothes, folded neatly, with his wallet, phone, and car keys not far from where he parked on the road. I'll have to go back and do some more tracking, but it smells like he was followed into the woods. Someone must have known his routine."

"And that he was a werewolf," Cal said, voicing what Simon must have been thinking.

"Aye, it seems that way," Simon said with a sigh. "I'll sniff around a bit more and see what turns up."

"Thanks Simon," Cal said. "I'll head home and start calling the others. We need to warn everyone that there may be someone hunting us."

Simon made a growling sound in the affirmative and hung up. Calvin stood frozen with his phone in a white knuckled grip still held to his ear. I stepped forward and reached up to touch his hand.

"Cal?" I asked.

His eyes were still closed, but he flinched and began to slowly open them. I once read an ostrich will hide its head to avoid seeing danger. Calvin appeared to be doing something similar. Unfortunately danger wasn't something you could avoid by keeping your eyes shut. *I should know.*

"Come on," I said, holding his hand. "Let's go sit down in your truck. We can come up with a plan and if you're too freaked out to drive I'll call Emma. She can come pick us up."

Calvin nodded, but his eyes were unfocused and I could tell he was in shock. He let me lead him to his truck where I grabbed the spare key and opened his door. He stepped inside and sat behind the wheel while I raced around to the passenger door and climbed into the truck cab. *What should I do now?*

I sat there awash in wet dog smell wondering what I could possibly do to help. Over the past few weeks I had noticed Calvin gave off the smell more when he was stressed. Seeing the picture of a dead man definitely ranked high on the stress meter. I just hoped Cal could retain enough control to remain in human form. His alpha status and Simon's training helped, but that didn't change the fact that many of the Old Blood shifted during times of extreme duress.

Cal already had a close call with shifting into wolf form on school grounds. During the Homecoming dance I had made the mistake of letting loose on the dance floor which inadvertently called out to Calvin's wolf spirit. He had begun to transform right there in the school gymnasium and we only managed to escape with the help of our best friend Emma. *But not everyone escaped unscathed.*

Cal had been injured, breaking his arm or foreleg as it was at the time, and though he was healing quickly I could tell his arm was still tender. The worst wounds from that night weren't physical. We all blamed ourselves for what happened and none of us would easily forget the events of Homecoming and the disaster only barely averted. I had promised myself I would never let something like that happen again, but I wasn't sure what to do next. I was supposed to be the anchor that kept Cal from losing touch with his human self. We were soul mates. *Soul mates.*

I suddenly knew what to do. I reached down and dragged my backpack up onto the bench seat. Pulling out books and notepads I found what I was looking for. I lifted a half-eaten sandwich from the plastic bag and jumped out of the truck. I peeled the bread away, letting the cheese fall with a slap to the pavement, and started crumbling and tossing the bread in a circle around the truck. I wasn't sure if this would work, but I would take all the help we could get. *Not really feeling choosy.*

A few weeks ago, while training with Simon, I had learned crows have a special relationship with wolves. In the wild, crows will lead wolves to a food source and have been known to warn them of danger. I didn't know if the crows could help if the danger to Cal happened to be his own wolf spirit, but my frenzied brain logic thought it was worth a shot. I continued to scatter bread in a circle around Cal's truck. When I ran out of bread I tried to think of some other offering. I looked down at myself and smiled. Crows like shiny objects. I stood in front of Calvin's truck with my arms open wide, sun shining on my metal shirt. It was a good day for being covered in safety pins.

"Yuki?" Cal asked.

His voice was coming from behind me and for a moment I wondered if I'd imagined it. I had closed my eyes against the sun and was reciting a mantra of "help Cal" and visualizing a flock of crows coming to his aid.

"Is there a reason why you're standing out there like that?" he asked. "If you're pretending to be a scarecrow, it's not working."

I opened my eyes and turned around to see Calvin looking at me quizzically. We were surrounded by crows feeding on the bread crumbs I had scattered. I approached Cal's window and leaned in for a hug. He didn't smell like wet dog. I felt so elated I twirled around singing, "shiny, shiny, crows are led, by safety pins, and bits of bread!" Cal just looked at me and laughed. *Hooray for frenzied brain logic.*

Our moment of gaiety was over too soon. There were storm clouds on the horizon, one filled with spirits of the dead and the other containing a person angry or disturbed enough to kill a member of Cal's pack in cold blood, and running away would only be a temporary solution. No, this was a storm we had to face head on.

I joined Cal inside the truck and together we dealt with the difficult task of deciding what to do next. I looked away, suddenly engrossed in the movement of one lone crow eating the remaining crumbs from the ground, as Calvin opened his phone to look at the wolf picture one more time. With a decisive nod he closed the phone and started the engine.

"Can you call Emma and ask her to meet us back at the cabin?" he asked. "Tell her we'll be there in about twenty minutes and to bring her supplies."

"Sure," I answered, already pulling out my phone.

"Need anything from your house?" he asked. "A change of clothes maybe?"

I could see Cal eyeing my safety pin shirt with amusement. If he thought I was changing out of my shiny shirt, he could think again. It was my new lucky shirt. *I might never change my shirt again.*

"Well, actually I could use my power boots," I answered. "I can run in and grab them and leave a note for my parents that I might be a bit late coming home tonight."

"Good idea," he said, already backing out of the school parking lot.

I speed dialed Emma and she answered on the first ring. "Girl, is everything okay?" Emma asked. "I just had the creepiest thing happen. I stopped by the veterinary clinic to check this week's work schedule and when I was holding Duvet, our resident boa constrictor, he *spoke* to me. He said you were in trouble."

A storm definitely was on the horizon. *When it rains it pours.*

Chapter 3

Cal and I had arrived at the cabin after raiding his parents' house for food. Emma was on her way and promised to bring her alternative medicines and medical reference books. We were all hoping we wouldn't need them, but had learned it was best to be prepared. I had also come to trust the prophetic words of our spirit guides. The spirits had always advised me in my dreams, but that didn't mean what Emma said wasn't true. I trusted Emma with my life, she had saved Calvin's once already, and if she said a snake told her I was in trouble I was inclined to believe her.

Cal and I settled in the mismatched armchairs and spread our notepads, pens, and phone books over the coffee table. It felt better to have a plan and be doing something. We decided the best strategy was to make a list of all the pack members we knew and to start calling them. I suggested we ask every member we call to in turn call all members they had contact information for. It wasn't a perfect plan. Some people were going to receive a lot of phone calls tonight, but it was better than missing someone. We needed to turn this situation around. The pack needed to be made aware of the possible danger. With awareness comes strength. We had to believe that.

"You guys are like contagious or something," Emma blurted as she pushed through the cabin door. Cal walked over to help carry her bags of supplies while I set aside the list we had been working on.

"Contagious?" I asked. "Do we have boy-girl germs?" *Didn't we grow out of cooties in middle school?*

"I'm serious," Emma said, looking back and forth between us. "Your weird abilities are rubbing off."

"Why don't you sit down and tell us about it while I put the kettle on," Cal said. "I think we could all use some tea."

"Amen to that," I said with a sigh. There was a lot of work ahead. I needed caffeine. *Lots and lots of caffeine.*

"Well, like I was telling Yuki on the phone," Emma said, "I drove to the veterinary clinic after school to check the new work schedule and while I was there I stopped to play with Duvet our new boa constrictor."

"Let me guess, Gordy named Duvet right?" I asked.

Gordy was Emma's new boyfriend and my long-time friend from anime club. Emma had asked Gordy to the recent Homecoming dance and they had been attached at the lips ever since. Gordy was a good friend, but we hadn't told him about my ability to smell the dead or about how Cal turns furry at the full moon. *Some things were best left unsaid.*

"How'd you know that?" Emma asked. "He was with me when they brought her in. As soon as she was identified as an adult boa constrictor he wanted to name her Duvet. Why? Does it mean something?"

"It's kind of an anime thing," I said. "The opening theme song for the anime Serial Experiments Lain is Duvet by Boa. Gordy probably couldn't resist the reference. Did he put his hands over his mouth and start saying 'Layer One' in a weird Darth Vader voice?"

"Unfortunately yes," Emma said, starting to laugh. "All the dogs started barking and my supervisor had to ask him to leave."

That was Gordy. The eternal goofball. *Some things never change.*

"So when you picked up Duvet today something happened?" Cal asked, carrying over our steaming mugs of tea.

"Yeah, something happened all right," she answered. "I was holding Duvet and she just started talking, but not really with her mouth. It was like someone was beaming the thoughts into my head. She said Yuki was in danger. You believe me don't you?"

"I smell dead people and my boyfriend's a werewolf," I said, rolling my eyes. "Of course I believe you."

"Did she say anything else?" Cal asked.

"No, she just went back to being a normal snake," Emma answered. "No more voices after that, but it doesn't lessen the creep factor. I don't know how you two deal with it all the time, but you can keep the crazy to yourselves. I've had enough."

"Good luck with that," I said, blowing across the top of my tea. "Anyway, we have bigger fish to fry."

"Did you have to say that?" Emma asked with an exaggerated shudder. "The poor little fish!"

She may have had a brush with the paranormal, but Emma was still Emma. *Some things never change.*

I was beginning to feel thankful for that. My life was changing so fast, and so many things were out of my control, I felt like the leaf swept up by the wind which swirls dizzily in mini tornadoes of someone else's making. The storm winds may shake me, and at times even force me to dance to their chaotic tune, but Calvin and his wolf spirit would be my shield and Emma would keep me grounded to reality. Emma was the root and branch that held me in place.

The cabin door opened and Simon shook himself, splattering rain drops all over Emma, and leaving his wet hair sticking out in all directions. *So not good.* Simon was one of the Old Ones, yet unusual for his kind. He had been born with an awareness of his wolf spirit, something which usually developed as the human host matured, which left him a bit...off. Simon had a slightly feral look in his eye and a wildness which didn't go away as the new moon neared, but his closeness to his spirit wolf gave him insight and wisdom which far exceeded his years. Not that he was young. Simon was in his late thirties, something I never failed to remind him of. Unfortunately that didn't mean he was overly mature. Simon and Emma never missed a chance to argue over the most trivial thing.

"I guess it's true what they say about the inability to teach old dogs new tricks," Emma said archly. "I see you haven't house trained this one yet."

Emma turned her back on Simon and missed the look of pure fury which raged across his face. It only lasted a second, but for that moment there was nothing human in his glare. He gained control of his wolf quickly though and shrugged, flicking more water on Emma, a slow predatory grin sliding across his handsome face.

"Is there a reason you smell like reptiles today?" Simon asked, looking steadily at Emma. "Something you'd like to share with the class? Finally found life forms as cold blooded as yourself?"

Son of a dung beetle. If someone didn't nip this in the bud, they would go on like this all night. "Emma had an experience with a snake," I said. "She was just telling us about it."

"Sounds kinky," Simon said, still grinning.

"That's enough," Calvin said. "We have important work to do and I need your report."

To my surprise Simon obeyed. I was still getting used to Cal's alpha status and what that meant. Simon often acted in the role of our teacher, but when it came to direct orders from Cal he listened. You hear about some people being born leaders, but in Cal's case it was true. He had been born with the spirit of the alpha wolf inside of him which meant he led the pack. Now that the pack was being threatened I could see the full weight of that responsibility in the dark smudges and tightness around his eyes.

"We know who our victim is, or was, and what he was doing in the woods," Simon said. "It looks like someone knew Gavin's routine and followed him once he shifted into wolf form. Poor man never even knew what hit him."

"How was he killed?" Calvin asked. "Do we have any idea?"

"Blow to the head," Simon answered. "But that's where it gets weird. First, it's hard to sneak up on one of us. Second, I smelled a werewolf, other than Gavin, there at the scene."

"What?" Cal asked incredulously. "That doesn't even make sense."

"Wait, it gets even more bizarre," Simon said, pulling a plastic bag from his pocket. "These items were under the body."

Body. I felt like I was going to be sick. I tried not to picture the wolf from Cal's phone, but the image was permanently etched into my brain. *Think happy thoughts, think happy thoughts.*

"You may want to get your girlfriend a glass of water," Simon said to Cal. "I like my girls pale, but she's beginning to look a bit green. No offense, love."

"None taken Old Man," I wanted to quip, but a sudden roaring in my ears was distracting me and I had the nagging feeling opening my mouth was a bad idea.

"Yuki?" Cal asked, reaching over and squeezing my hand. "You alright?"

"Help her put her head between her knees," Emma instructed.

Cal rubbed my back as I stuck my head between my knees. Great. Now all eyes were on me and I looked like a freak...or a turtle. *Teenage Mutant Ninja Freak.*

"Go ahead you guys," I mumbled, waving a hand for them to continue. "Don't mind me." *Nothing to see here.*

"Okay kitten, if you insist," Simon said.

I felt Cal growl as it rippled down his arm and through the hand which still rested on my back. "What's in the bag?" Cal asked, his voice deadly serious.

Simon blinked at the plastic bag in his hands and set it on the coffee table. "Found these bits beneath the body," Simon said. "Seems our killer is a nutter. Joe Schmoe sociopath. He left some weird religious odds and ends. I'd bet a dance with the devil that bullet and cross are made of silver."

My curiosity won out over my nausea and I pulled myself back to a sitting position so I could see the contents of the bag. The bag was clear plastic and nestled inside were what looked to be a silver bullet, metal cross, and an assortment of dead plants.

"This guy has issues," Emma said. "Issues plural. Definitely not a werewolf lover that's for sure."

"Our man is quite the wolf hater," Simon agreed.

Simon and Emma never agreed on anything, ever, but the items did seem to fit the profile of someone with a deep hatred for werewolves. "So the attack wasn't random," Calvin said and sighed.

"He wasn't shot was he?" I asked.

"No the bludgeoning was quite adequate to ensure his death sweetheart," Simon answered.

I ignored his teasing and pushed on. "So the bullet is just symbolic then," I said. I wasn't sure if it was important, but I wanted to understand what each of the items meant to the killer. Maybe the items in the bag could help lead us to him.

"That's a good point," Cal said. "What are the other items? Are those plants?"

Emma leaned forward for a closer look and froze, only her eyes continued moving to look up at Simon. "Simon, did you touch any of these plants?" she asked.

"No darling, I'm not that naïve," Simon scoffed. "I know better than to touch evidence."

"Good, that knowledge probably saved your life," she said. "That piece of flowering plant is an aconite commonly known as Wolfsbane. It may be symbolic for repelling werewolves, but it is also a very toxic plant. Fatal doses of the poison can easily be absorbed through the skin."

Son of a dung beetle. This was getting way creepy. I felt like spiders were crawling under my skin. Even Simon looked disconcerted.

"This bit of leafy branch is from a Mountain Ash or Rowan tree," Emma said. "You may all recognize the last plant as mistletoe. Mistletoe can be poisonous if ingested, but I think what all of these items have in common are their symbolic uses as werewolf wards. Many werewolf superstitions include at least one of them."

"Maybe he just wanted the mistletoe for when he met pretty girls," Simon quipped. "All men can't be as devastatingly handsome as me."

I just rolled my eyes at Simon, but Emma looked ready for a fight. Fortunately Calvin chose that moment to take control and tell them about our plan. He assigned each of us a list of names and instructed us on what to say when we called. We wanted to avoid mass panic, and we had to be careful to only speak about the Old Blood to actual members of the pack. It wouldn't do to tell the human babysitter that a raging, murderous, psychopath werewolf was on the loose. *I don't think she'd take the news very well.*

Each of us found a dry place to settle in with our cell phone and list of names. Taking a deep breath I reached out and squeezed Cal's hand, our eyes meeting for just a moment, reassuring each other everything would be okay, but the reality was that things may never be okay again. The storm was coming. I had less than two weeks to prepare for the bombardment of angry spirits who threatened to drive me insane, or worse, on Samhain, and a madman, probably a werewolf, was hunting the members of Calvin's pack. Cal, my friends and I were needed to stop the loss of more life. I felt a cold sliver of fear. We were running short on days before Samhain and couldn't tackle more than one problem at a time. I hoped that we found this killer soon so we could get back to working on solving my predicament. Thunder rolled in the distance, lightning flashed, and rain began drumming hard against the cabin roof. *Not usually a good sign.*

Bad omens and bitter portents. It was going to be a long night.

Chapter 4

October 21st Maine

*I*t was the beginning of a new day. The storm had cleared and the sun was shining in a cloudless sky. Rain and high winds had torn freshly turned autumn leaves from the trees and the newly carpeted lawn resembled an orange, brown, and red patchwork quilt. I reached my hand to the glass pane of my bedroom window and let the cold seep into the pads of my fingers.

Fall had always been my favorite time of year. A time for candy apples, cool breezes, and curling up with a good book. The chill of the glass pane was a reminder that soon it would be time to huddle inside our homes for the long Maine winter. I always longed for those first few weeks of winter snow when everything outside is blanketed in white, a hushed silence descends, and we all feel safe in the comfort of our warm hearths and homes.

As I pulled my hand away from the window I set bells jangling on their string. I had placed them across my window a few weeks ago when I was worried about the retribution of an old lady I suspected of murdering her husband. Grace hadn't sought revenge, I don't think she ever became aware of my role in helping her husband's spirit find peace, but the bells remained. I often felt as though someone was watching me and now there was a murderer on the loose. I shivered and turned from the window. I don't think I'll ever feel safe in my home again. *Well that's positive thinking Yuki. Way to start the day.*

If I was going to feel gloomy I might as well get ready for school. I grabbed my backpack and, with a sigh, began loading it up with notebooks, pens, and our lists from last night. Pulling on arm warmers and wrapping a scarf around my neck I surveyed my room. What else would I need to survive a day of high school? Removing my phone from its charger I slipped it into my coat pocket. Glancing back, I decided to bring the charger as well. I wasn't sure when I'd be home next. Heading down the stairs to the front door, I turned sharply to the left, my bag swinging wide, and made a quick detour to the kitchen. Opening the pantry door I scanned the shelves for food. This could be another *very* long day.

I ran to the front door when I heard a truck horn beep once in the driveway. *Cal.* My heart swelled and my stomach began dancing a tango. I zipped up my backpack, checked the locks, and went to face the one wonderful part of my day.

I couldn't help the grin that stretched across my face as I climbed up into Calvin's truck. I knew we had things to be worried about and it probably was somehow taboo to be so incredibly happy, if only for this brief moment, when people were frightened and a man's family was so freshly mourning his loss. The logical part of my brain thought about these things, and even tried to school my face into a mask of solemnity, but my heart had other plans. As I leaned in close to Cal I could see the marks of worry and lack of sleep in the lines of his face and the dark bruised circles beneath his eyes, but as I smiled at him his eyes shone with an inner light and his lips curled up in a breathtaking grin.

"Morning Princess," Cal said as his warm lips brushed mine. His hands cupped the back of my head and I reached up to lace my fingers behind his neck. I closed my eyes as we kissed, floating in my own little world of happy.

As we pressed closer together, I felt the heavy iron cross I was wearing press hard against my chest just as Calvin mumbled, "Ouch!"

"Sorry," I said, trying to refocus.

"And this is for?" Calvin asked, lifting the offending cross.

"Spirits, demons, creatures of the night," I answered. "Why? It didn't burn you did it?" I asked teasingly.

"I fear I have passed your test," Cal answered, raising his hands to his chest in mock horror. "Whatever shall the other night creatures think?"

"You totally just lost your monster street cred," I said.

"I thought you were going to wear your safety pin shirt every day," Cal said. "Where's your lucky chain mail?"

"I can't wear it *every* day," I answered. "I have to wash it occasionally. Otherwise it would be gross. I don't want to smell like a boy."

"Boys everywhere take offense to that," Cal said, grinning.

"They can get in line," I said. I laughed and, shifting my cross pendant to the side, leaned in for another kiss before we had to drive to school and leave our cocoon of laughter and sunlight.

*****

The school day dragged and lunchtime couldn't come soon enough. The events of the previous day weighed on my mind and my backpack seemed to grow heavier as I hauled it through the halls between each class. *Maybe I shouldn't have brought that five pound bag of trail mix.*

I tried to summon a bit of enthusiasm as, lifting my bag higher on my shoulder, I walked to the cafeteria trying not to drag my booted feet. My pace quickened as I smelled the glorious aroma of warm brownies.

"Someone's baking brownies!" I exclaimed as I sat across from Emma at the lunch table.

"If that's a euphemism for bodily functions, it is so not funny," Emma said, crossing her arms.

"Dude, don't you smell that?" I asked. "It's making me hungry."

"Well, if they *are* making brownies I won't be able to eat them anyway," Emma said with a sigh. "It's not like they'd bother to make them vegan."

"How do you make them vegan?" I asked suddenly curious. "Don't you need eggs and butter?"

"No way," Emma answered. "You just use applesauce instead. No embryonic chickens or dairy products necessary."

I suddenly didn't feel much like eating brownies. Fortunately for me whoever was doing the baking must have left them in the oven too long and the smell of burning brownies diminished my urge for chocolate. "Smells like you won't be tempted by the evil death brownies after all," I said, wrinkling my nose. "Not unless you like them extra crispy."

"What's extra crispy?" Cal asked as he slid into the seat beside me.

"Burnt brownies," I answered. "Can't you smell them?"

"Yuki, my sense of smell is pretty amazing and all I smell is chop suey and gym socks," Cal said.

Spending lunch with my friends was turning into a great diet plan.

"It's probably just one of her ghost buddies," Emma said, looking over at Calvin.

Son of a dung beetle. "Not again," I groaned, putting my head in my hands.

"At least it doesn't smell like vinegar," Emma said encouragingly.

Oh yeah, what an improvement. Burning brownies smell just super. I was in Hell and someone had been thoughtful enough to bring the brownie mix. *Fantastic.*

"I wonder...," Cal mumbled quietly, looking thoughtful.

"You wonder what?" I asked. "If you're wondering why I, of all people, have to be haunted by smell impressions, don't strain your brain. I have that market cornered."

Cal blinked and looked back and forth between me and Emma. "Did that make any sense?" he asked. I kicked him playfully under the table which seemed to jog his memory. "I was wondering if this smell impression could belong to the ghost of Gavin Sanders. He just died and may be attached to you because of your involvement with the case."

"And it's not like Maine is a hotbed of violent crime," Emma added.

Emma and Cal were probably right. It was entirely possible Gavin's spirit had found me. I was a total ghost magnet, much to my chagrin. There was no real evidence though to my new haunt's identity. Until I had more details, I wasn't ruling anything out. Looks like I was going to have to put some of my newly learned research skills to work.

"So what's the plan for after school?" I asked. "Anyone up for some research at the library?"

Emma's eyes lit up at the mention of research, but then she sighed looking a bit deflated. "I have a shift at the veterinary clinic today, but I can drop you off on my way to work and join you guys later if you're still doing research." She started to cheer up again at the prospect of hitting the stacks after work. Emma was a total research addict.

"I was going to meet up with Simon and check out the woods where they found Gavin," Cal said. "Last night's storm probably erased any evidence, but I'd still like to get a look at the location. Maybe there's something about the place that Simon missed."

I was suddenly very excited at the prospect of doing research *inside* the library. Cal was the outdoorsy one, not me, and I could totally skip sniffing around the spot where someone died. *Where a man was murdered.*

"Perfect," I said, smiling. "Emma can drop me off at the library and meet back up with me after her shift ends."

Emma looked at me and nodded excitedly. "I am so there," she said. "I'll even sneak us in some soy lattes. Just be sure to get us the third floor study area."

"Are you sure you don't need me?" Cal asked. "I feel bad taking off with Simon, but I keep worrying he may have missed something or that there might be something in the woods I'm meant to see." He looked at me worriedly and I melted.

"Don't worry," I said. "Emma and I can handle the research."

"Girl power, yo," Emma said, knocking her knuckles to mine.

"I give up," Cal said, laughing.

"Just promise to be careful," I said to Cal, squeezing his hand and pushing my leg playfully against his.

"Always am," he said, grinning.

"Promise?" I asked.

"I promise," Cal answered. Brushing my hair back behind my ear, he leaned closer and whispered, "I love you."

I forgot all about spirits and haunting and werewolf murderers and melted into a puddle of contentment. *I love you too Calvin Miller.*

Chapter 5

Emma dropped me off at the library after school as promised. She waved as she pulled away in her mom's minivan. Her car was being detailed in an effort to remove the dirt and blood stains from Homecoming night. I had given her the money I had saved from my birthday, but I still felt guilty. She said it was no big deal. Her mom was even pitching in since Emma had told her we had rescued an injured dog and transported it in the backseat of her car. It wasn't a total lie. We *had* transported a canine, but ours had bigger teeth and claws than the average dog and, oh yeah, happened to be my boyfriend.

The smell of burning brownies suddenly engulfed me and I turned to walk up the damp, leaf covered steps of the library. Nothing like an unquiet spirit haunting me as a personal motivator.

As I reached the top step, I heard the call of a crow, *caw caw*, and the flutter of wings. Feeling the hair on the back of my neck stand up and my scalp prickle, I nonchalantly tossed my scarf over one shoulder and turned to look behind me. I thought I saw movement, but as my eyes scanned the sidewalk and street below I could find nothing out of place. Great, now I'm jumping at every flicker of shadow. *Thanks a lot crow dude.*

Turning again to the library entrance I reached for the door, but it was already swinging outwards. I quickly jumped back and was glad for my non skid boots or I would have slipped on the wet steps. I still had to grab hold of the metal railing to keep my balance so I didn't see the jerk pushing past, but I grumbled "excuse me" to his retreating back. Some people were just beyond rude. *Let's try this again.*

This time when I cautiously reached for the door there were no crow alerts or crazy stampedes. I walked into the hushed silence of the library and set off to secure a cubicle in the third floor study area.

*****

Two hours of research had turned up zilch on any burning brownie death connections. I had scoured the local obituaries and news stories, online and microfiche, for reports of dead bakers or someone murdered for their inheritance to a brownie empire. I even looked for articles on home and restaurant fires, but there was nothing involving fatalities. The smell of burning brownies, for the moment, seemed to be a dead end. *Har, har, har.*

I turned my attention to information on how to ward off evil spirits. I found some promising titles listed and went in search of a librarian. Emma was the queen of research, but I was still learning and wasn't too proud to ask for help. When I approached the desk on the first floor I was greeted by an overly perky girl with frizzy red hair and a painfully frozen smile. *At least she's trying to be friendly*, I thought as I showed her my list, *unlike some people*. I was still mad about the guy who nearly knocked me down the library steps.

"You're in luck!" said the girl. "I can help you find most of these. Spirit wards and werewolf wards must be popular this time of year. Halloween and all."

I stood stunned for a moment before I could remember how to speak. "Someone was interested in werewolf wards?" I asked. My voice broke, but the girl didn't seem to notice.

"We just had a guy in here earlier asking for all of our books on werewolf wards," she said. "When you asked for these books on spirit wards the very same day I figured it was for some kind of Halloween project."

"Uh, yeah," I said. "Did he check any books out?"

Please, please, please. If he checked books out there would be a paper trail. There would be a name.

"Nope," the girl answered. "He just asked to see the books and then put them back on the cart when he was done."

"Are they still on the cart?" I asked.

"They're right over there," she said, waving her hand towards a wheeled cart. "We haven't reshelved them yet."

I started to head over to the cart and felt a hand on my arm. I nearly jumped a foot.

"Sorry," the girl said, looking abashed. "I didn't want to shout, but I wondered if you still want these?"

She was holding up my list of books on spirit wards. "Oh yeah, sorry," I said. "Could you bring them up to the third floor study area? I don't think I can carry everything."

"Sure," she said. "We're here to serve!"

Her cheerfulness was beginning to grate on my already frayed nerves, but I tried to smile since she was doing me a favor. "Thanks," I said and turned to the cart. I was bombarded by the smell of burning brownies and prayed silently that she didn't notice my hands shaking as I stacked the werewolf books and carried them up the stairs. Could that guy have been the werewolf murderer? Perhaps the crow was right to warn me after all.

*****

When Emma arrived I was still researching spirit wards, but kept the pile of werewolf books within sight. I was hoping Calvin or Simon might be able to sniff out some clues. *Literally.* I had texted Cal about an hour ago and he texted back that they would drive back to town and meet us at the library before closing time. I had been sneaking looks at my watch ever since.

"Girl, you look like hell," Emma said, setting a tall soy latte on the table. "Here, drink this."

I drank a huge gulp of creamy caffeine goodness and sighed. "I so needed this," I said. "Thanks."

"No problemo," Emma said. "So what are you working on?"

"Actually big problemo," I said. "Huge, epic even."

Emma raised an eyebrow and crossed her arms. "You can't leave me hanging like that," she said. "There's a law against it, I swear."

"I'm allowed an exaggerated pause," I said, *pausing*. "I think I came face to face with the killer. Actually it was more like face to door...or door to face."

"Where?" Emma asked excitedly.

"Here, in front of the library," I answered. "He nearly knocked me over at the entrance when I was on my way in."

"The entrance I just walked through?" Emma asked nervously.

"Yeah, that's the one," I answered.

"Well that's all kinds of creepy," Emma said with a shudder.

Tell me about it. "He was researching werewolf wards, like the items left at the murder scene," I said. "I grabbed the books he was looking through and brought them up here. I sent Cal a message and he's on his way here to, uh, take a look at them."

"Well, if he needs to do his wolf thing first then I won't touch them," Emma said. "After Cal's done though, we should really find out what's in those books. It might help us find this guy."

"Do you have room on your library card to check them out?" I asked.

"Are you kidding?" she asked. "Mine is totally maxed out. Is Simon coming with Cal?"

"Yeah, I think so," I answered.

"Then we should make him check them out," Emma said. "That is, if he even has a library card."

To Emma that was the biggest insult ever. She worshipped this place. Books were her religion and the library her church.

"I'm sure Simon has a library card," I said. "He's not a total spawn of Satan. He just likes to pretend he is."

"Talking about me again darlings?" Simon asked as he rounded the corner to our study area. "You can stop going through Simon withdrawal loves. I'm here now in the flesh."

"I take that back," I said, looking at Emma. "He really *is* the spawn of Satan."

"There's really only one way to find out," Emma said. "Simon, do you have a library card?"

"I think it's in my pocket," Simon said, grinning at Emma. "Want to help me search for it?"

"Simon," Calvin growled, walking toward us. "Enough!"

Simon pulled his wallet from his back pants pocket and, eyes downcast, slid his library card onto the table in front of Emma. He turned his back to Calvin and winked at Emma with a huge grin on his face. *Brat.*

The sly grin slipped from Simon's face as he began sniffing at the air. Walking closer to the stack of books at the corner of the table, he exclaimed, "The illegitimate son of a...he's been here. The man I smelled in the woods at the murder scene. He handled these books."

Son of a dung beetle. My hunch was right. The guy who nearly knocked me down the library steps was our murder suspect. A tiny voice inside my head wished I could have pulled off some hardcore ninja moves when I had my chance, but it was a very, very small voice. Mostly I felt afraid. I was afraid of the killer who lurked in our midst, for my friends and the safety of the pack, for myself, but most of all afraid for Calvin, the love of my life and the most likely target for a man obsessed with hunting werewolves.

Simon's affirmation of the man's presence at yesterday's murder scene left us all a bit out of sorts. Calvin sat pensively staring at the offending stack of books; Emma turned an ashen shade of gray and opened the nearest book on spirit wards, escaping into her well-ordered world of research; and Simon paced like a caged animal. I looked down at my already chewed black fingernails and tried not to think about blood and brownies and the glassy eye of a wolf who could no longer see this world.

"When is the funeral?" I finally asked. "I should probably be there in case this new spirit really is Gavin."

"It's scheduled for the day after tomorrow," Cal said. "You're right. We should all try to attend. Maybe the killer will even make an appearance. Do you think you'd recognize him?"

"I don't think so," I said. "I really didn't see his face, but the spirits might be able to give me something. It's worth a try."

Cal knew how much I cringed at the thought of funerals and cemeteries, where I might encounter more spirits of the dead, and gave me an encouraging smile. "Thanks," he said. "I'll be there with you the whole time." *My knight in furry armor.*

"Don't thank me yet," I said ruefully. "I still may run screaming from the funeral which would *not* be helpful. Too bad I can't wear my safety pin shirt."

"Why not?" Emma asked. "Shiny is the new black."

"Says who, love?" Simon asked dubiously.

"Says me," Emma hissed.

I was so not looking forward to this funeral and Simon and Emma's arguing was only making my headache worse. The acrid smell of burning brownies wasn't helping either.

"You two better start getting along if you're going to pass as each other's date for the funeral," Cal said.

"What?" Simon and Emma asked in unison.

"You have got to be kidding me," Emma added.

"Actually it makes a lot of sense," I said. "We don't want to arouse suspicion. Going as couples, rather than as a group, is the logical thing to do. Right Cal?"

"Right," Cal said.

28

It would also mean I may even have a few minutes of peace and quiet for the drive over to the cemetery. Emma was shooting me daggers, but right now I was much more concerned about keeping my sanity. I wasn't kidding about potentially freaking out at the funeral. In my world funeral homes, graveyards, cemeteries, and hospitals were the stuff of nightmares. There tends to be a concentration of spirit activity in these places and I had discovered it was best to avoid such areas.

Now I was planning on jumping from the frying pan right into the fire. Not my best plan ever, but what's a girl to do? My friends were in danger and I was willing to take the risk if it meant I could save more lives. Heck, consider it a preemptive strike on the creation of more spirits. It was a logical, strategic plan of action, right? *Then why do I feel like I have enormous vampire bats fluttering around my stomach?*

Chapter 6

*C*al had ordered Simon to go with Emma and carry the stack of werewolf books to the van for her. He was still at the counter flirting with the ever smiling redhead as Calvin and I ducked out the front. Cal was carrying the books on spirit wards, but still managed to hold the door for me. *Always the gentleman.*

The chill night air felt soothing on my face and I hoped I wasn't getting a fever. The headaches were bad enough. I definitely didn't need a cold to slow me down. I could smell wet leaves and wood smoke and realized the burning brownie smell had lessened. Perhaps my ghost was taking a nap? Did spirits sleep? If so, what did they dream about?

"Penny for your thoughts," Cal said quietly. There was something about the empty rain dampened street that invited silence though his whispering may have been a side effect of too much library time.

"I was wondering if ghosts ever sleep," I said with forced jocularity. My voice sounded harsh and thunderous and I mentally tuned myself down a notch or three. "If androids dream of electric sheep, does that mean ghosts dream of spectral livestock?"

"If I followed your logic, then I'd dream of chasing sheep rather than counting them," Cal said. *He had a point.* "Which reminds me, I'm starving. Want to stop for a bite? Maybe I can find some lamb chops."

"That's baaaaaaad," I joked.

Cal groaned and led the way to his truck. After depositing the books safely behind his seat he walked around to open the passenger door for me. I tossed my overburdened backpack onto the passenger floor and turned back to Cal. Looking up at him, his head a halo of golden light beneath the streetlight, I reached up and gave him a kiss. My angel may have teeth and claws, but he was an angel all the same.

*****

After picking up take-out Thai food, Cal drove me home. I was about to invite him inside when I noticed my parents' cars were both in the driveway. I hadn't realized how late it had become.

"See you at school tomorrow?" I asked.

"Most definitely," Cal answered. "Need a ride?"

"Most definitely," I said, leaning in for one last goodnight kiss.

When we finally came up for air, Cal jumped out and retrieved the books from behind his seat. I was feeling dreamy and had forgotten all about them. He carried the books to the front door and helped me get them inside before leaving.

"Goodnight Yuki," Cal whispered. "Sweet dreams."

I closed the door behind him and turned the lock. The house was dark and quiet so I tiptoed up the stairs to my room, juggling the books and my bag of take-out food, while trying not to bump into anything. I was largely unsuccessful, but my parents didn't come out into the hall so I figured they were still asleep. I felt my way to the bed and when my shins hit the mattress I dumped the books onto the comforter. Walking back to flick on the light I listened again for my parents, but they didn't stir. Perhaps they were dreaming of sheep?

My stomach growled out loud and I quietly clicked my door shut and brought the bag of food over to my desk. I pulled out fresh spring rolls and crispy tofu with peanut sauce and was suddenly ravenous. I couldn't remember the last time I ate anything other than trail mix. Pictures of dead wolves and the smell of burning brownies had a tendency to make me lose my appetite.

Stomach appeased, I turned to the pile of books on my bed. One cover had a charcoal sketch of a brooding spirit gazing out from the cover. "Don't look at me like that," I muttered, deciding to read that one last. I picked a smaller book with Celtic knotwork and vines on the cover and set it on the nightstand. Lifting the rest to the floor, I plunked down on the bed and unlaced my boots. I leaned back against the headboard and settled in for a long night of reading.

*****

At some point in the night I must have drifted off to sleep because I now stood in an unfamiliar fog shrouded forest. The mist covered ground made walking treacherous. Roots grasped at my feet and ankles and cobwebs clung to my face and hair. What was this place?

I tried not to wonder what was hiding in the darkness. It wasn't working. My mind conjured up images of nightmare creatures and I began to run. My logical mind screamed that running was a bad idea and would only attract the attention of lurking monsters, but my feet flew across the fog covered ground. I ran and ran until I tripped and fell face first into water.

Flailing in the water I awoke wrestling with my sheets and gasping for breath. I tried to remember any details from the dream which may have been important. I hadn't been visited by any spirit guides. Maybe it had just been a regular nightmare brought on by stress. The feeling of terror clung to me though, and I reached for my notes on warding off evil spirits. Looks like I was going to have to go carve myself a turnip. *Seriously, don't ask.*

Giving up on sleep entirely I slid on my skelly slippers and crept downstairs to the kitchen. I looked through the pantry shelves and refrigerator drawers, but didn't turn up any turnips. My sleep deprived brain seemed to be turning to bad puns for amusement. *Fun, fun, fun.* Glancing around the kitchen my gaze fell on a bowl of decorative gourds. Bingo.

The book I read on spirit wards claimed people would carve turnips or gourds with faces to confuse evil spirits. On Samhain they would light these curiously carved veggies with candles and either carry them or set them in their windows for protection.

I selected a few small gourds and began carving faces. When my mom padded into the kitchen an hour later I was putting on the finishing touches.

"You're up early sweetie," she said, stifling a yawn. "Big day at school?"

"Halloween art project," I replied. "I kind of forgot about it until last minute. Hope you don't mind I used some of your gourds," I said gesturing to the nearly empty bowl. "I'll buy some new ones today after school. I promise."

"Oh, don't worry," she said, waving her hand in the air. "I'm just glad someone gets to enjoy them. We're hardly ever home lately anyway."

"Thanks mom," I said. "Want me to put the coffee on?

"That sounds lovely, but first what is the dark green one supposed to be?" she asked. "A spider?"

"Yeah," I answered excitedly. "Look, I made a little harness so he can sit on my shoulder. See, like this. His legs dangle and bounce around. Isn't he cute?"

"He's adorable," she said, smiling. "Now where's that coffee?"

"Coming right up!" I said.

I wore my spider the entire time and purposefully made the legs bounce and swing around as I reached for the mugs and ground the beans, which made my mom laugh. It looked like my little friend really could scare away evil spirits. Things seemed brighter already.

Chapter 7

I was putting the finishing touches on my ensemble when I heard the crunch of gravel announcing Calvin's arrival. Checking in the mirror I was pleased with the overall look. I had added white face powder to my already pale complexion and lots of black eyeliner to frame my eyes. I was wearing all black and my spider gourd was perched on my shoulder. I also had a little white pumpkin which I carved to look like a ghost. Before leaving for work my mom had threaded a black ribbon through two holes carved on the sides so I could carry it like a purse. A little battery votive candle flickered inside making its eyes shift back and forth. I felt ridiculously happy as I skipped down the stairs and out to Calvin's truck.

I climbed into the passenger seat careful not to jostle my spider. Cal looked at me quizzically, but then began to laugh.

"Just when I start to worry about you Yuki, you do something to prove to me just how strong you are," he said.

"Strong?" I asked. "Don't you mean silly, weird, wacky? I could go on."

"Nope, not silly," Cal said. "Yesterday you seemed depressed and I was worried that everything going on was just too much, but seeing you today I'm impressed. You look so happy and it makes me happy. I don't know how you do it. You amaze me."

You amaze me. With three little words Calvin could make me melt.

"It's the power of the gourds," I said, giggling. "Pumpkin power."

"There's a story there, isn't there?" Cal asked.

"I got the idea from one of the library books on spirit wards," I answered. "Back in the day, like way old school, there was this custom to carve turnips with faces and light them with a candle to ward off harmful spirits on Samhain."

"Like jack-o'-lanterns?" Cal asked.

"Yeah, that's where the tradition came from," I said. "Later they started carving gourds instead of turnips and pumpkins became popular here in America. But the belief was that carrying these lanterns would keep the evil spirits away."

"So that's why you have a ghost gourd purse and spider gourd pet on your shoulder?" he asked.

"Well, that and they're totally cute," I answered, batting my eyelashes.

"On you, anything is cute," Cal said, leaning in for a kiss.

*****

Not everyone in school agreed with Calvin. I received some nasty looks and stares as I walked the hall to class. I heard more than one cheerleader titter, "witch" and point at me. *Whatever.*

"Bit early for Halloween isn't it, witch?" asked Jared Zempter, sneering.

Ugh! Just what I needed, the almighty J-team trying to ruin my day. Well, I wasn't going let them spoil my good mood. Jared was a bully who was only nice to other jocks and cheerleader bimbettes. He had a nasty cruel streak and, oh yeah, he hated me. Jared, and his clone Jay Freeman, had been trying to make my life miserable ever since a ridiculous mishap in gym class freshman year. It didn't matter that I had nothing to do with Jared falling on his face like an idiot. I tended to sit out when

36

the jocks were getting all sweaty and had been sitting on a bench nearby when Jared tripped over his own shoelace. His friend Jay noticed the evil eye pendant I was wearing and so, naturally, blamed me. They'd been calling me a witch ever since. *I so can't wait for high school to be over.*

"You know you just have a nasty case of gourd envy," I said confidently and continued to walk to class.

Without his full entourage to explain to him what that meant he just fisted his hands in frustration and glared at me as I walked away. There is one good thing about the J-team. They are not very smart. *Brains will win out over brawn every time baby.*

*****

"Oh my gourd!" Emma exclaimed. "Those are so cute!"

Oh no, the bad puns were contagious. "Thanks, I carved them this morning," I said.

"Have you named them yet?" she asked.

"I was thinking Legs and Boo, but I'm up for suggestions," I said.

"I like Legs and Boo," she said. "They are too cute and totally you."

"Thanks," I said. "One of the books I checked out of the library said these will help to ward off harmful spirits. There used to be a tradition of carrying them on Samhain."

"Really?" she asked. "That's awesome."

"Yeah, even wearing masks and costumes for Halloween comes from the belief it confuses the evil spirits that come out Samhain night," I said. "Reading all of that old lore made me wonder if there were more people like me back then. People who were, you know, sensitive to spirits."

"Was there anything in that book about giving out candy?" she asked.

"Not candy exactly, but they did used to have these huge feasts," I answered. "Samhain was a festival of the harvest and of the dead. Oh, and there was something called guising where kids would go door to door wearing costumes and masks and carrying their lanterns. People would give them apples and nuts and sometimes coins, but I didn't read anything about candy. Why?"

"I knew it," Emma said smugly. "It's all a modern day conspiracy brought on by the candy corporations. I wanted to give out healthy snacks for Halloween, but do you know how difficult that is? There was this whole mass media freak out over razor blades in apples, so now if you give out fruit people think you're crazy."

"So what are you going to do?" I asked.

"I'm giving out those little boxes of raisins," she said. "They're individually packaged and sealed so there's no way I put razor blades in them."

"So you're giving out zombie grapes," I said.

"Yeah," Emma said.

"Cool," I said, forcing a smile. "I wish I could stay home on Halloween and give out zombie grapes."

"Oh hun, that was totally insensitive," Emma said. "I was forgetting about how stressful this really is. Don't forget I'm there for you. I'll even give up my plot against candy corporations and spend the night with you instead. We'll figure something out."

"Have I mentioned lately how much I love you?" I asked, getting teary. "Crap, my mascara is getting all smudgy." I tried to blink my eyes rapidly to dry my lashes.

"It just adds to the look," Emma said with a wink. "Very dramatic."

"Thanks," I said.

"Don't look now, but your boyfriend is on his way over here," she said.

"Why shouldn't I look?" I asked.

"Because his tray is loaded with nearly every species in the animal kingdom," she said with exaggerated disgust.

Emma was a hardcore vegan, but she knew Calvin was a werewolf and therefore a meat eater. She had confessed to me she had actually come to accept that Cal's carnivore tendencies were part of the natural order of things, but she still liked to give him a hard time. Emma loved a good argument.

I could tell Cal was stressed before I even saw him approach. The smell of wet dog was a dead giveaway. No wonder his tray was piled with meat. Cal worked hard to maintain self control, but under duress his wolf spirit came closer to the surface.

"Everything okay?" I asked.

Cal set his tray on the table and ran his hands through his shaggy hair. He took a deep breath, in and out, before sitting down beside me. I could tell he was trying to compose himself before speaking. *Not good.*

I sat quietly stirring my yogurt, feeling my good mood slip into the whirlpool within. Calvin was always easygoing. Something major must have happened for him to look this rattled. Even Emma knew when to leave well enough alone. The silence was oppressive and the smell of burning brownies was suddenly suffocating.

"Has there been another murder?" I asked.

Cal let out a sigh and looked at me with haunted eyes. "We don't know yet, but I'm worried," he answered. "One of our pack members is missing. His sister called me since we left word to report anything unusual. She said she wouldn't even be worried yet if it wasn't for the recent murder."

"Have you called Simon?" I asked.

Simon may be annoying and a terrible flirt, but he had proven himself to be resourceful in the past. He had also been working with Calvin, helping him to control and communicate with his wolf spirit. If things became more stressful, Cal was going to need every ounce of control to keep his wolf spirit from taking over.

"I called him just a minute ago," he answered. "He said he'd have my dad call the school to release me early today. I'm meeting with Simon at the cabin and then we'll try to visit the places Sam usually hangs out. His name is Sam, by the way."

"How old is he?" Emma asked.

"He's our age," Cal said, staring at his food tray. "On second thought, I don't think I'm hungry after all." He stood up and emptied his tray in the nearby trash bin. As he was setting the tray on the counter an announcement came over the intercom calling him to the office. Stuffing his hands in his pockets he walked back to our table and leaned down to kiss me on the forehead.

"Call me after school?" he asked.

"Absolutely," I answered. "Should we all meet at the cabin?"

"I'm not sure what time Simon and I will be getting back," he said. "Can we make plans later?"

"Sure," I said. "Good luck."

Cal nodded and walked away. I hoped that Sam was just out having fun. Maybe he stayed out late with friends or went for a run in the woods. Werewolves his age often needed to shift more often and it's hard to phone home when you're in wolf form. *Please let this be a false alarm.*

"Yuki?" Emma asked. "Earth to Yuki."

"Huh?" I asked, still deep in thought.

"You can stop stirring your yogurt," she said. "Most of it's on the table now anyway."

"Oops," I said. I had slopped yogurt all over the table in front of me.

"I'll go get paper towels," she said, getting up to leave. *Too bad all messes can't be cleaned up that easily.*

By the time Emma returned with wet paper towels my mood had improved. The smell of wet dog and burning brownies had retreated with Calvin and I suddenly had the urge to do something productive after school.

"Do you volunteer at the shelter today?" I asked. Emma worked a few shifts now at the veterinary hospital, but I knew she still volunteered at the animal shelter.

"I'm free today," she answered.

"Want to come over and teach me how to make vegan cookies?" I asked.

"I thought you'd never ask," she said laughing. "We can have cookies ready for when the guys get back from their search. I bet they'll be hungry."

"Absolutely," I said, smiling.

Just then the bell rang and we had to run to class. I swung Boo on her ribbon and Legs bounced around on my shoulder as I rushed down the hall. *Who could stay sad when they had Legs and Boo?*

Chapter 8

*S*topping to collect Cal's missed assignments from his teachers made me a few minutes late meeting Emma in the school parking lot. I looked around for her mom's minivan, but didn't see it anywhere. I was starting to worry when a huge SUV pulled out to reveal Emma standing smugly against her car. *Her car!* I ran over, Legs and Boo bouncing, and wrapped her up in a hug.

"Oh em gees!" I exclaimed. "Your car. It's alive!" The last I said in my best doctor Frankenstein impersonation.

Emma laughed and gestured to the passenger door. "Get in," she said.

I opened the door to the smell of upholstery cleaner and bubblegum scented air freshener. I settled into the newly cleaned seat and, with trepidation, glanced into the back seat. *Please let the blood be gone. Please, please, please.* There were no stains on the gray fabric and the seat belts had been replaced. I released a breath I hadn't realized I was holding.

"The car looks great," I said as Emma got in behind the wheel.

"Thanks," she said. "I just got it back this morning. Feels good to be driving my own car and not my mom's gas guzzling monstrosity."

"Where to?" I asked.

"My place," she replied. "You are so totally going to learn how to make vegan cookies."

I called Cal on the way to Emma's house, but got his voicemail. I left a message letting him know where we were going to be hanging out and wished him luck in his search.

"Voicemail?" Emma asked.

"Yeah, it's cool," I said. "Hard to answer the phone with paws!" I was trying for levity, but my words came out flat. *Awkward with a capital A.*

"Let's go make those cookies," Emma said, ignoring my weirdness. "I'm starved."

Walking into Emma's house meant stepping into a wild menagerie where humans were a minority. The first thing I always noticed in the dimly lit entryway was the sensation of being watched and then the gleam of many sets of eyes from the adjoining living room. There were animals of nearly every furred and feathered variety and they perched and lounged on every surface.

I nearly jumped when a paw swept down to bat at Legs' fabric legs. Many of the strays and injured animals Emma and her family fostered would eventually leave to return to the wild or go to a good family, but there were a few here who were long time family pets. The brave tom cat with one ear was one of these permanent fixtures in Emma's home.

"Hey Van Gogh, you like Legs?" I asked, reaching up to scratch the cat's good ear. I was nearly knocked off my feet by the other long-term resident, a huge Maine Coon cat with a jealous streak. "Don't worry Chairman Meow, you're next." I made sure to give them equal attention, scratching and cooing until they purred like motorcycle engines, and moved on toward the kitchen.

Emma was setting out ingredients and I went over to scrub my hands at the sink. Amazingly the animals of the house didn't cross into the kitchen. I wasn't sure if this was due to the slippery linoleum floor or training, but I was glad we wouldn't have to worry about pet fur in the cookies. *Then they wouldn't really be vegan, right?*

*****

We were already eating from the first tray of cookies and waiting for the second batch to cool when I received a call from Cal. He and Simon hadn't found the missing teen and were on their way back to town. We agreed to meet them at the cabin in thirty minutes.

Emma and I waited for the last cookies to cool and cleaned the kitchen. Her mom and dad would be home from work soon which was why we didn't invite the guys over to her house. Simon didn't play well with others. We left a plate of cookies wrapped in cling wrap on the kitchen table for her parents and a note explaining Emma would be back by eight o'clock. I hoped the cats would continue to stay out of the kitchen after we left. Chairman Meow might be getting a plate full of vegan cookies for dinner.

On the drive over to the cabin Emma was fidgeting at the wheel and seemed distracted. We had been laughing and having a good time while baking, but now she looked anxious and little worry lines were beginning to pop out on her forehead. I tried to remember if I had said anything to upset her, but was drawing a blank. I even liked her cookies and had told her so. Emma fuming wasn't good. I needed to do something to defuse the Emma bomb...*and fast.*

"So, are you okay?" I asked. I might as well be direct. We were only a few minutes from the cabin so I didn't have time for subtleties.

"Oh sure, if by okay you mean totally freaked out," she answered.

Okay. "Did I miss something?" I asked. "What's wrong?"

She sighed and put her turn signal on, pulling over to the side of the road. When we came to a complete stop she still held the steering wheel with a white knuckled grip. "Please tell me I'm not going crazy," she said.

"Whatever it is, you are not going crazy," I said. "You're one of the most sane people I know."

"Well, then why are snakes talking to me?" she asked. Emma turned to face me, her usual calm exterior shattered. "When I was locking up, as we were leaving the house, the snake in the terrarium by the door spoke to

45

me." She looked like she was going to be sick and her hands had started to shake.

"But I thought this happened once before at the clinic," I said. "No big. Really. This stuff happens to me all the time. Granted it usually happens in my dreams, but I think there's some weird metaphysical trickster who likes to mess with us and make us all experience these things a bit differently. I wouldn't worry about it though. You are not going crazy."

"When it had only happened once I thought I could just blow it off as a one shot trip to crazy land," she said. "But when it just happened again it was like...like being told that I'm now a part of this. Like no matter how much I want to go back to being normal I am going to stay like this. I...I guess I just wasn't ready for the big reveal."

"Yeah, I don't think any of us ever are," I said, reaching for her hand.

Emma gave my hand a quick squeeze, then pulled back to face the road. "You know what I could use right now?" she asked. "A good fight and a whole plate full of cookies."

I had been hoping to avoid one of Simon and Emma's explosive arguments, but if that was what would make her feel better right now then that was what she would get. *One big bad wolf coming right up.*

We arrived at the cabin a few minutes later and Emma marched in looking for a fight. I almost felt bad for Simon. *Almost.* Calvin and Emma were the only people there though when I walked inside.

"Where is he?" Emma asked, arms crossed and foot tapping.

Cal raised an eyebrow, but answered, "Simon shifted and went to check the perimeter. We need to be careful with the killer still out there somewhere and neither of us have been here all afternoon. He should be back soon."

"We baked cookies," I announced, waving the plate of oatmeal applesauce cookies.

"All for me?" Cal asked, jokingly. "Thanks!"

"No, not all for you," I said, laughing. "You have to share."

Cal slipped his arms around my waist and leaned in for a kiss. "Are you sure I can't have the whole plate?" he mumbled.

Nice try Calvin Miller. "Have...to...share," I mumbled.

He kissed the edge of my mouth and smiled. "Okay princess, may I have one cookie?" he asked.

"Sure," I answered as he ate the cookie in two bites. "It's vegan."

"What?" he asked and nearly choked. "You could have told me first."

Emma and I started giggling. "But then you never would have tried one," I said.

Cal pulled a funny face and pretended to choke making Emma laugh harder.

"Act like that and I'll make you eat the whole plate yourself," Emma threatened.

"Mwhahaha, my evil plan has succeeded!" Cal exclaimed. "Hand over the plate."

Emma and Cal ran around the cabin with the cookie plate. It was good to see them both laughing. *Just like old times.*

We all had a funeral to go to the following day so Emma and I left early. Simon hadn't returned yet, but Emma no longer seemed in need of an argument and I was too tired to deal with his annoying personality. We agreed to meet at Cal's parents' house in the morning. Our group would then split into two couples, me and Cal and Emma and Simon, so we could blend at the funeral. *Oh yeah, this was going to be fun.*

Chapter 9

October 23rd

I awoke to the rumble of thunder overhead. *Great, that bodes well.* I rolled out of bed and padded to the window. The sky was gray, with dark smudges of storm clouds in the distance, but it wasn't raining. *Yet.* I walked to the bathroom and flicked on the overhead light. My reflection stared back at me gloomily. I was wearing my retro Gremlins pajamas and Gizmo was giving me a thumbs up.

"Yeah yeah, I know, Gizzy is the shizzy," I mumbled at my reflection. I mirrored Gizmo's thumbs up and wandered off in search of food and caffeine.

Getting dressed should have been the easy part of my day. People wear black to funerals and I had a closet brimming full of black clothing. Easy right? Unfortunately I was also dressing for battle. Going to the funeral meant entering a cemetery where I would likely be bombarded with the smell impressions of its many ghostly residents. I was going to need every protection trick and spirit ward up my sleeve if I hoped to survive the day with my sanity intact. The hard part was that I really needed to literally fit these items up my sleeves. I could get away with a few crosses, but too much occult bling at a public funeral would draw the wrong kind of attention. We needed to be discreet, hence my wardrobe dilemma.

I set my chain mail for spirits down on the bed with a sigh. There was no way it was fitting under any of my nice blouses. I grabbed a belly chain that I had only been brave enough to wear once and attached a few charms to it, extra crosses, a silver four leaf clover, a Thai Buddha amulet, and a Seal of Solomon protection charm, and slipped it on. I grabbed a non-toxic magic marker and drew a few more crosses and symbols from the library books on my upper arms and stomach where they wouldn't show once I was fully dressed.

I pulled a black cami on first and my high necked ruffle blouse over that. I hooked my evil eye pendant around my neck and slipped the pendant under the blouse. I slipped my large ornate cross necklace over my head and let the cross rest on my blouse. It was goth, but not too over the top. I clipped a few tiny bells into my hair, then pulled on a floor length black skirt and laced up my boots. There were a few loose herbs in the toe of each boot, more spirit protection, and they tickled my stocking feet.

Thunder rattled my window and I decided to bring my waterproof trench coat and an umbrella. I shoved a few more charms into my coat pockets and, with a silent prayer, ran for the stairs. I felt the cold sliver of fear slide down my back. *Or was that just one of my charms?* Either way I had a bad feeling about this.

*****

Emma was waiting for me in the driveway and looked fabulous in her black dress. Emma normally only wore white, cream, or gray so it was a shock to see her alabaster skin and pale blond hair against the contrasting black of her dress.

"You look amazing," I said. She also looked older, but I wasn't going to mention that. I wondered if it was intentional. She was going as Simon's date after all.

"Thanks, you too," she said, getting into the driver's seat. "Are you jingling?"

"Um, yeah, that would be me," I said guiltily. "Is it that noticeable?"

"Not really," she answered. "You might just want to refrain from jumping up and down."

"Right, because people do that all the time at funerals," I said sarcastically.

"Fine, don't take my advice," she said primly.

What was her deal today? "You ready for some detective work?" I asked. "You and Simon can be like Holmes and Watson or Starsky and Hutch."

Emma shot me a look that would freeze lava. *Well at least I know what she's mad about.* If I hadn't been so focused on my own dread of today, then I would have realized just how uncomfortable Emma must be pretending to be Simon's date for the day. She was eighteen and he was *old.* I wasn't exactly sure how old, but he was probably in his thirties. *You know, ancient.*

"So I was wondering if maybe we should have a change in plan," I said. "You could give Simon a ride, but then split up when you get to the funeral. You don't really have to stay together."

Emma let out a sigh. "I would, but I have to admit that the boys have a point," she said. "We shouldn't go in there on our own. There's a killer prowling around and I, for one, don't want to be his next victim. No, we'll stick to the plan. The buddy system is the sensible thing to do."

"You could call Simon your 'buddy' all day," I suggested. "That would probably annoy him."

"I like that plan," she said. "I like that plan a lot."

*****

"Ah, there's the little lady," Simon said as we walked into Cal's parents' house. He swaggered over and put his arm around Emma. "Miss me, love? No worries, we get to spend the entire day together."

Simon was so totally a dead man.

"It's not wise to taunt your doctor," Emma said icily. "You wouldn't want me angry the next time I patch you up...or when you're sick and I make you drink my tea." Emma reached up and skillfully slipped out from under Simon's arm while placing her hand on his forehead. "Why Simon, are you running a fever? You may need my tea sooner than you think."

51

Simon blanched and looked uncertain. Emma had a level of power within the wolf pack, they were in need of her medical and veterinary skills, but up until now she had only made Simon drink her tea. An experience he obviously didn't want to repeat. *Ever.* What Emma was doing now was establishing her rank in the hierarchy and Simon seemed unsure of how to proceed. She wasn't one of the Old Blood so they couldn't fight for dominance, which only seemed to leave a battle of wits and wills, and Emma was very, very good at arguing. Simon seemed to size her up then stepped away.

"Fine, doc, whatever," he muttered. "Can we get this show on the road? We have a killer to find and a brother to mourn."

"Ready?" Cal asked.

It suddenly occurred to me he hadn't said a word or stepped in when Emma and Simon were having their power struggle. He let them work things out on their own and Emma had come out on top.

"Ready," I said.

Now that I didn't have to worry about Emma, I had my own problems to obsess over. Emma and Simon left in her car while Cal and I pulled away in his truck.

The ride to the cemetery was the longest ten minutes of my life. When we reached the wrought iron cemetery gates I tried, and failed, to repress a shudder. The sky overhead had darkened and as I looked past the stone walls, to the row upon row of grave stones, I couldn't help imagining the spectral images of wailing ghosts and hand wringing spirits around every stone and monument. I really needed to lay off the scary movies. My mind was conjuring up horrifying images and I wasn't sure if this was some form of coping mechanism or a slow descent into madness. Maybe I should just stay here in the truck. *Yeah, that's it. I'll just stay here on the nice safe street in the safety of Cal's truck.*

Cal's fingers reaching out to hold my hand nearly made me faint in terror. *Oh yeah, it's official, I am totally freaking out.*

"You don't have to go in," Cal said. He was looking at me with such open concern that my breath turned into a hiccupping sob. *No. I was not going to cry. Not today.*

"Yes, I do," I said. "I may be able to divine something from the smell impressions. And…and it probably isn't even safe out here by myself."

I didn't like admitting that last part. I preferred to think of myself as tough and self-reliant, but the reality was that a killer with supernatural strength was stalking the Old Blood and possibly those closest to them. I was also a mess. I was stressed out and sleep deprived and jumping at shadows. Entering the cemetery may not be on my list of favorite ways to spend the day, but it was what I needed to do. Hopefully I wouldn't commit any funeral faux pas like hyperventilating, flailing at the air, or running screaming through the cemetery. Fingers crossed. *Toes too.*

Cal was holding my hand, but I still managed to jingle along with my jangling nerves. I just couldn't stop fidgeting.

"I've got charms that jingle jangle jingle," I sang quietly to myself.

"Are you singing?" Cal asked quietly. He was smiling which was a good thing. At least, I hoped it was a good thing. I sure as heck prayed it wasn't the smile that came before calling the men with straightjackets. *They're coming to take me away, ha ha, they're coming to take me away.*

"Sorry, nervous habit," I said. I felt like I was speaking too rapidly, a sharp staccato that sounded harsh to my ears, and the smell of burning brownies was increasing.

Cal must have sensed my growing unease because he gathered me into his arms and held me tight. The smell that was Cal, woods, wet dog, fresh air, and warm skin, washed over me and I began to feel safe.

"I'll be with you the whole time," Cal said into my hair. "I won't leave you. You don't have to face this alone."

As we sat there in Cal's truck people were streaming in through the cemetery gates and walking up the narrow path to the group of mourners gathered at the top of the hill. *Time to face the music.*

"Okay, let's do it," I said, pulling away. I reached for the door handle and felt the cold metal beneath my skin. *I can do this. I am strong. I am me. No wispy flesh and blood wannabe is going to take that away. Not today.*

Stepping around the truck, Cal reached for my hand and we walked together across the street to the cemetery gate. I felt a breath of cold air and a slight popping in my ears as we crossed the threshold. That was when all Hell broke loose.

It is very, very difficult to be the only person experiencing raw terror and knowing that you have to appear like everything is just fine. The situation was so far away from fine we had traveled to another galaxy.

Normally I can only sense the dead through smell. It's an annoying gift and it sucks, but I always guessed there would be something much worse if I ever dared venture past the cemetery gates. I was right. There was a roaring in my ears and a piercing headache forming behind my temples. My face felt like it was being touched by cold tendrils brushing past as I walked, one step at a time, up the gravel path. It was confusing and disorienting and I held on to Cal, knowing that he wouldn't let me fall.

Oh and the smells! I was bombarded with smells from every direction. The smells came in every form; acrid, pungent, sweet, floral, each and every one of them stirring up memories and feelings. It felt like a violation, but it wasn't like I could stop breathing. *Oh yeah, and I had to act normal.*

Somehow we managed to run the gauntlet and made it to the gathering at the top of the hill. I was breathing rapidly and hoped that anyone who noticed assumed it was from exertion. As we came to a halt amongst the mourners I caught a flash of Simon's grin and Emma's blond hair, but then the crowd shifted. I realized belatedly they were making room for Calvin. He was the pack alpha after all. We were moved to the front, closest to the newly turned earth, Cal holding my hand in a vice-like grip.

My ears were ringing too loudly to make out what was being said and the funeral itself passed in random flashes. A woman's shoes. Blink. Gazing around the circle of downcast faces. Blink. A tuft of grass longer than the rest. Blink. A handkerchief edged with embroidered roses. Blink. The only constant was the barrage of odors and the ever present smell of burning brownies.

At one point I thought I saw Emma reach out for Simon's hand, but I had to be imagining things, right? After hours, or minutes, the crowd began to disperse. Cal exchanged a few words with whom I assumed must be the grieving widow, but as promised he never left my side. My headache was pounding, the roaring in my ears deafening, and I was beginning to lose feeling in my legs when Cal steered me towards the gates. I stumbled down the path, with Cal holding me upright, and nearly wept with relief when we cleared the cemetery gate. I wanted to bend down and kiss the ground, but wasn't sure if I could get back up again. Plus there was the whole trying to look normal thing. Instead Cal helped me into the truck where he wrapped me in a blanket, turned up the heat, and held me until I stopped shaking. If this was what it was like to be exposed to one small cemetery of ghosts, then I was totally unprepared for Samhain which was only a week away. I might as well start picking out the straightjacket now. *Do you think they come in black?*

*****

55

Attending the funeral after-party was much easier than the graveside ceremony. Fewer spirits, more werewolves. *My kind of party.* They all looked human in their black finery, but there was something less controlled in their actions here. I assumed it was similar to what I had experienced at Wolf Camp. Here, among their own kind, there was nothing to hide.

When Cal and I entered the room all eyes turned to us, or rather to Calvin. At his nod though everyone seemed to relax and go back to mingling and eating and drinking. What was it about death that made people want to eat? Was it an attempt to fill the empty hole in their lives or something to do with endorphins? I'd have to ask Emma. She would know. Emma knows everything food related. Looking at the table, filled with casseroles and desserts, I suddenly had an epiphany. I knew how I was going to work the subject of burning brownies into conversation. I guess the cemetery hadn't totally fried my brain. *Good to know.*

I grabbed a slip of paper from my coat pocket and mimed writing. After searching through his pockets Cal handed me a pen and I wrote an abbreviated version of my plan. Why was I writing notes to my boyfriend when he was standing right there? Well, werewolves have more sensitive hearing than humans and I didn't want to risk having my plan overheard. After just a few seconds I had communicated my plan to Cal and he moved away toward the refreshment table.

With more than a bit of trepidation I approached the grieving widow. Okay, honestly I was pretty uncomfortable with this, and the growing smell of burning brownies wasn't helping any, but I had just faced one of my worst fears and survived. How bad could subterfuge be? Oh right, have I mentioned how much I suck at lying? I could feel my face burning red with embarrassment as I stepped up to Mrs. Sanders.

"Hi Mrs. Sanders, I'm Yuki," I stuttered. *I'm the head case who was hyperventilating at your husband's funeral.* "I came with Cal."

"Thank you for coming," she said. Her eyes were red-rimmed from crying which made what I was about to do ten times harder.

"I feel really bad," I said. "I mean…I feel bad I didn't bring anything to eat. I made brownies, but I ended up burning the entire batch. I guess I should have left the baking to Cal." I held my breath waiting for her reaction. I didn't have to wait long.

Her smile wavered and her eyes flooded with tears. "Oh, burnt brownies would have been appropriate," she said, shakily. "They were Gavin's signature dessert. He made them every weekend. We joked he burned them on purpose just so he could smother them in vanilla ice cream. They were inedible otherwise and we always kept ice cream in the freezer for when he would bake his brownies. I guess I don't need to buy as much ice cream anymore…" Her voice trailed off and I took that as my cue to leave. I had the information that I needed.

"I'm so sorry for your loss," I mumbled, backing away.

As I crossed the room to where Cal was standing, someone lifted their glass and began a toast in Gavin's memory. It was unbelievably sad. He obviously had been a really nice guy, a nice guy who would never again be coming home and baking brownies with his family. My thoughts turned to Sam, the missing boy our own age, and I sent up a silent prayer that he was still alive.

When I reached Cal he held out his hand and led me to the door. The cool outside air and sunshine on my face was invigorating and I felt like I was waking from a bad dream. As we climbed into Calvin's truck my stomach growled out loud. Funny, I hadn't felt hungry at all while surrounded by food inside, but now that Cal and I were alone I was starving.

"I hope pizza sounds good, because I told Simon and Emma that we'd meet them at the Leaning Tower of Pizza downtown," Cal said, smiling.

Pizza? Heck yes. I needed to get away from thoughts of madness, death, and murder and feel some sense of normalcy. Going out for pizza with my boyfriend, best friend, and Simon was as close to normal as my life gets. Plus, I was starving. Maybe there was something to funerals making you hungry after all.

"I knew there was a reason why I fell in love with you," I said, grinning.

Cal leaned over, his eyes half closed, lips moist, and said throatily, "And here I thought it was my kissing."

"Mmmm...that would be reason number one," I said. Our lips met and our bodies melted together. *Oh yeah, definitely reason number one.*

*****

Cal and I arrived at the Leaning Tower of Pizza a few minutes late. *What can I say?* My hair was tousled and I had lost many of the small bells from my updo, but my hair wasn't quite as wild looking as Cal's. His hair was always shaggy, but I had been running my hands through it while kissing and now it looked like he had stuck his finger into an electric outlet. I thought about saying something, but he just looked so adorable.

Emma and Simon were sitting in a corner booth and we hurried to join them. I was immediately aware of the seating arrangement. Emma and Simon were both sitting on the same red vinyl bench seat leaving the opposite side of the table for me and Cal. It wouldn't have seemed so strange if they were any other two people on the planet, but Emma and Simon couldn't stand each other. They nearly scratched each other's eyes out every time they were in the same room together and, though Emma had established the upper hand earlier in the day, I was sure that their battle for dominance wasn't over. I wondered again if they really had been holding hands at the funeral. Emma had a lot of explaining to do.

"You two look awfully cozy," I said, lightly. "Something happen at the funeral?"

Cal raised one eyebrow, but didn't say anything.

"She finally succumbed to the Simon charm is all," Simon quipped. "It was bound to happen eventually. I *am* irresistible."

"You are so full of it," Emma said, leaning her head back against the padded booth and closing her eyes. "I have the most horrendous migraine. Yuki, how do you deal with having these all the time?"

"The threat of drinking your headache ease tea usually keeps them at bay," I said. "But you never get headaches. Any idea what triggered it?"

"Yeah, talking snake," Emma said with a sigh. *Oh.*

"Looks like your friend will be joining us for training," Simon said, smiling at me slyly. "The things some girls will do to get my attention." He winked. "Of course, I'll be deeply wounded if she just sits back and falls asleep during our sessions."

"Oh shut *up*," Emma said exasperatedly. "I am not falling asleep. I'm resting my eyes since they feel like they're about to mutiny and jump out of my skull. And I am not taking sleep insults from a guy who has to turn in circles before he can lay down for a nap."

Simon growled in response, but turned his attention to the menu. Emma continued to rest her eyes while a satisfied grin spread across her face. *Interesting.* I never witnessed a person so effectively trade insults with their eyes closed. It was kind of impressive.

We decided on one extra large meat lover's pizza for the guys, a personal veggie and cheese pizza for me, and bread sticks for Emma. Pizza is one of the reasons I could never go vegan. I have to have my cheese. Emma tried to make a case against the guy's pizza by explaining the origins of sausage, but Simon just mumbled something about "yummy lips and gizzards" around a mouthful of pizza. Emma went back to nibbling her bread sticks in disdain. Once we had all stuffed ourselves I turned my attention back to Emma.

"So, the suspense is killing me," I said. "What did the snake say to you today?"

"It said that the missing boy, Sam, was underground, but still alive," she said. "That's good news, right?"

Calvin and Simon exchanged a look, but didn't say anything. *What, do they have telepathy now or something?* My mind conjured up images of being buried alive, but I shrugged it off. Emma's spirit guide had said Sam was alive and underground, not buried alive, so there was no reason to jump to macabre assumptions. *Way too much Edgar Allan Poe as a kid.*

"That's definitely good news," I said. "Any other clues?"

"No, he just said he was underground," she answered.

"We'll get the word out to pay special attention to basements and caves," Cal said.

"Someone should check the sewers as well," Simon added. "What? Don't shoot the messenger."

"No, you're right," Cal said. "We'll put together search teams and draw straws to see who gets the sewers."

I winced at the thought of trudging through the town's sewer tunnels. *I thought I had it bad with smells.*

Chapter 10

I was exhausted from my ordeal at the cemetery and Emma continued to suffer with a migraine headache so Cal agreed to drive us home early. Simon volunteered to follow us in Emma's car and leave it at her house. Cal and Simon planned to work late coordinating the search parties.

When we finally reached my house Cal waited until I was safely inside before driving away. I sat on the bottom stair, building up the strength to climb up to my room, and unlaced my boots. Pieces of dried flowers and herbs trailed out as I pulled off each boot. Grabbing my boots in one hand and my coat in the other I stomped up the stairs.

I was agonizingly tired, but the memory of cold spirit fingers on my face and the smell of hundreds of ghostly smells entering my head made me stop in the bathroom and run a steaming hot tub of water. I poured in a heaping scoop of sandalwood bubble bath and stared at the growing mass of suds. I had an antique claw foot tub in my bathroom, which I always thought was extremely cool, but right now I was regretting the extra high sides that I had to climb over. *Oh well, no time like the present.* The tub wasn't getting any shorter nor the water any warmer. I peeled off my clothes and sank into the bubble filled water. My arms were the only thing above water, besides the top of my head, and I was startled to see the large black crosses and sigils I had drawn on each arm in stark relief against my pale white skin. I started scrubbing them with a loofah, but they wouldn't budge.

Son of a dung beetle. Leave it to me to use a permanent marker.

When the water was only lukewarm and my hands shriveled like raisins I finally dragged myself out of the bathroom to flop on my bed. I picked up one of the library books from the stack and decided to research spirit wards some more. There had to be something in these books that could help me survive Samhain.

I was reading excerpts from the Ulster Cycle, Irish mythology filled with heroic tales, and an analysis of the historical interaction of the Sidhe, or fairies, with spirits of the dead. In these old stories the Sidhe had the power to rule over the spirits and demons that were set loose on the night of Samhain. Now if I could just find a fairy to protect me on Samhain...yeah, like that's going to happen. Not a likely scenario, but I added it to my wish list.

I looked for more information on the Sidhe, but didn't like what I found. Fairies weren't cute glittery girls with wings. They were terrifying monsters who lurked in the shadows searching for mortals to torment. The more I read about the Sidhe the more I didn't ever want to cross paths with one. I'd rather take my chances with the spirits of the dead.

I read tale after tale of the bloody history of the Sidhe. My hope was that I would learn how they managed to control the spirits of the dead on Samhain. Was it an innate power combined with their own immortality, or was there an item or ritual that they used?

The legend that I came back to over and over again was the Echtra Nerai, The Adventure of Nera, from the Ulster Cycle. The story was a fascinating one. During a feast on Samhain, king Ailill proposed a test of bravery. He offered up his golden sword as reward to any man with courage enough to go out into the demon and spirit plagued Samhain night and tie a circle of twigs around the ankle of one of the men hanged the day before. To win the sword the man must do this and return to the king's feast hall. Though many men tried they all were attacked by demons and spirits and came fleeing back to the feast hall unsuccessful, all except for one man, Nera from Connacht. Nera braved the spirit filled night and tied the circle of twigs to the ankle of the hanging dead man.

At this point the story got weird or, well, weirder. The corpse became animated and Nera, for some reason I hadn't quite worked out yet, ended up carrying the dead man around on his back. I so hoped that wasn't the magical way to survive the spirits of the dead. I did not want to carry around a smelly corpse all night. *No. Way.*

Anyway, while he was giving the animated corpse a piggyback ride around town, it asked for water so Nera carried it to a house, but the house burst into flames. The next house they tried was surrounded by a moat of water that they couldn't cross. When they approached the third house they were finally able to enter and the corpse drank three cups of water, but then spit the last few sips of water on the people living there which killed them. Again, not real clear on the water spitting of death, but that's what the stories all said.

This was where the different versions and translations of the story diverged. Some claimed that Nera went willingly to the underground kingdom of the Sidhe, while other accounts say that he was taken prisoner, and other stories said that he was either aided on that night by a Sidhe woman, or that he stole something from her. Whether he was said to stay with the Sidhe for a year, willingly or not, or if he only had the one interaction, the story always ends with Nera surviving the spirits of the dead and successfully returning to the feast hall of the king. More than one account bragged that Nera stole, or was given, a treasured item of the Sidhe. What if this item was what helped him survive the spirits of the dead?

So much for sleep tonight. I crept down to the kitchen and turned the coffee maker on. The smell of freshly brewed coffee flooded the room, blending with the ever present odor of burning brownies. I grabbed my mug and stuck it under the stream of coffee. *Don't try this at home kids.* As soon as I had a full mug I carried it back upstairs and turned on my computer.

I now could narrow my focus to items the hero Nera may have taken from the Sidhe. I grabbed my notebook and pen and settled in for a long night of searching. The probability of figuring out what the item was, if it even existed, was not good and the odds of being able to locate it were even worse, but I tried to remain hopeful. The power of positive thinking and all that, right? But even I wasn't prepared for what I found.

Chapter 11

October 24th

*I*just may survive Samhain after all. The idea was intoxicating. I was also a bit giddy from lack of sleep, so I began my day laughing maniacally. I would have made a good stand-in for any mad scientist. *Dr. Frankenstein eat your heart out.*

Today wasn't a school day which meant I could have slept in if I had fallen asleep at all, but Emma had sent me a text asking to come over early and I eagerly accepted. I couldn't wait to tell her about what my research had uncovered. I pulled on a clean black cami top, black paratrooper pants, and my 14-eye doc martens. I layered a black mesh top over the cami and grabbed a hoodie for later. I wanted to be prepared in case we joined the search teams this afternoon. My hair was a nightmare, I really should have combed it last night before it dried, so I split it down the middle and tied it into braids. Looking in the mirror I was pleased at my reflection. The magic marker crosses on my arms were a nice touch. Laura Croft meets Wednesday Addams.

I was just finishing attaching a row of safety pins to my arm warmers when there was a knock on my bedroom door. Emma came in two seconds later looking like she hadn't had much more sleep than I did. She shuffled over to the bed where she dropped into a slouch. Was she sick? Emma always had perfect posture. *Always.*

"You okay?" I asked.

"I think I have a problem," she answered.

"The snake thing?" I asked. "We can work on that together and I'm sure we can get Simon to include you in our lessons. You'd be surprised at how much he knows about working with spirit. Once you learn to control it better, the headaches shouldn't be as bad."

"That's...good, but talking snakes actually isn't the problem I meant," she said. "I have boy problems."

Son of a dung beetle.

"Did Gordy do something?" I asked. "If so, Cal will totally talk to him." *He's so dead.*

"No, he hasn't done anything," Emma answered, quickly. "In a way, that's part of the problem. He never does anything. It's always the same thing with Gordy. Watch anime in the media room after school or go to the movies on the weekend. I feel bad, but I'm just so bored."

"Well, I was kind of surprised when you two hooked up," I said. "Gordy's a great guy, as a friend, but he's not all that exciting. He's not on the same level as you Emma. You're all about being proactive and he's just not. You two did seem to have some chemistry though."

"I know," she said. "It was fun at first. I tried giving us some space this week to see if I missed him, but I think getting space just made me want more space."

"I noticed you two weren't spending a lot of time together this week," I said. "I just thought it was due to the werewolf killer, talking snake, spirit ward search stuff. It's not like you can invite Gordy to come with. He doesn't even know these things exist outside of anime."

"Yeah, that's part of the problem too," she said. "All of my concerns these days are about if my friend will go crazy from a spirit attack, or if my other friend will get jumped by some psycho werewolf killer, meanwhile I'm obsessing over snakes talking directly into my brain and I can't share *any* of it with Gordy. When I'm with him I just sit there counting the seconds until I can leave. That's just not fair to him...or to me."

"If you aren't happy, then make a quick, clean break," I said. "Gordy's too good of a friend to string along."

66

"You won't be mad if I break up with him?" she asked. "You were friends first."

"No way," I said. "I'd be mad if you stayed with someone who didn't make you happy. You've only been dating for a few weeks and you're already feeling bored and guilty. Just think of how unhappy you'd be a year from now."

Emma jumped up and gave me a quick hug. "You're the best!" she said. "I feel better already."

"You do?" I asked.

"Absolutely," she answered.

"Good, because we have work to do," I said, grinning.

*****

When I told Emma about discovering Nera's amulet as a potential ward against the spirits coming on Samhain, she couldn't wait to visit the library for more research. She drove us there like it was a matter of life and death. *Perhaps it was.*

The library's stone and brick edifice had never been such a welcome sight. I took the steps two at a time and nearly leapt through the front door. My enthusiasm was contagious and Emma was grinning from ear to ear as she caught the door behind me.

"Ready to find your amulet?" she asked.

"Oh yeah," I answered. "I was born ready."

I was still in my tough girl outfit and feeling the warm glimmer of hope building inside my chest. I could feel a wild smile spread across my face to match Emma's frenzied grin. *Maybe that's why everyone is inching away.*

Stifling the hysterical laugh rising in my throat, I slipped into the stacks. I felt as though the answer to my salvation was just on the periphery. If I were fast enough and smart enough, I could catch it and survive Samhain. It was an empowering feeling and I wondered idly if this was how Cal felt when he was following a scent trail. I was on the hunt for Nera's amulet and the trail of clues was leading me to unexpected places. *Very unexpected.*

During my initial search for information on Nera's amulet I was surprised to see old sketches and ancient carvings that looked vaguely familiar. The more I stared at images of the amulet the stronger the nagging sensation that I had seen it before. After my tenth cup of coffee, I finally remembered where. *Could it really be that close?*

I didn't want to get my hopes up, only to have them dashed on the rocks of reality, so I enlisted the help of Emma, researcher extraordinaire. If we could find more evidence to link the amulet I had seen with Nera's legendary amulet, then I would begin to breathe easy and bust out my happy dance. Well, not a happy *dance*. No way was I risking accidentally calling out Cal's wolf spirit. If there was reason for celebration, my happy feet would just have to settle for jumping for joy.

With arms heavily laden with books, Emma and I clomped up to the third floor study area. Our usual cubical was available, not many people were in the library first thing Saturday morning, and began sorting through the books we had found. Whoever had the unlucky task of shelving these was going to have their hands full. We had books from numerous sections including archaeology and ancient artifacts, Celtic and Gaedhilic mythology, history of the Salem Witch Trials, and goldsmithing and the art of jewelry making. Emma even had an auction catalog.

Why gather information on the Salem Witch Trials? The connection was tenuous at best, but the place I was sure I had seen the amulet, like the one used by Nera, was in an occult shop in Salem Massachusetts. If I remembered correctly, the amulet was in a glass case, on display as a historical piece. Now I just had to find out if they really were one and the same.

"Why the books on jewelry making?" Emma asked, raising one eyebrow. *Was I the only person incapable of doing that?* Whenever I attempted to raise one eyebrow I looked like I was trying to join both brows to my hairline. *So not fair.*

"If the amulet in Salem really is Nera's, then it won't be for sale," I answered. "The shop owners had it on display to attract visitors, like a museum piece, so I may have to...borrow it." This was the part that made my stomach churn and palms sweat.

"Wait a minute, didn't you say the shop was owned by witches?" Emma asked.

"Yeah," I said, shakily.

"So if this is the right amulet, you're going to go steal it from a bunch of witches?" she asked.

"That's the plan so far," I said, nodding slowly. "But if I do have to take it, I'm going to leave a replica in its place. Maybe they won't even notice."

Okay, I knew this was wishful thinking, but it was the best I could come up with. We were growing short on time and the spirit storm front was moving closer. I was diametrically opposed to stealing in principal, but I was even more against the idea of death and insanity. *Blame it on the rain.*

"Right," she said, pushing the goldsmithing books to the side and rolling her eyes. "Let's hope it doesn't come to that. I've seen your art projects and, girl, you are no Michelangelo."

"Great," I said. "Thanks for the vote of confidence." *Like I needed another reason to freak out.* I really didn't want to be turned into a toad. They eat flies. *Gag me.*

"Just keepin' it real," she said, nose already in a text.

*****

After three hours and eleven minutes of research, not that I was counting, we dragged ourselves to the photocopier. I fed the machine money while Emma made copies of any pictures we had found of Nera's magic amulet. When we finished I lugged the books to the returns cart and we walked to the media lab.

Finding an available computer we searched for the shop in Salem where I had last seen the amulet. Unfortunately I could picture the exact layout of the store, but couldn't remember the shop name. Unless it was called Dark and Spooky, we were in for a long search. Emma called up a map of downtown Salem and I tried to visualize walking the brick and cobbled pedestrian streets with Calvin last year.

Cal had always been into all things mystical which was what initially drew us to Salem years ago. We would visit the New Age shops, bookstores, and palm readers for Cal and then go shopping in the Goth clothing and accessory stores for me. Heck, I had found some of my favorite outfits in the year-round Halloween costume outlets.

I suddenly remembered going into a witches' apothecary shop that had these cool dark fairy prints in the window. Cal had gone to the back wall which was covered in small bags of dried herbs and other witchy ingredients. The reason the shop stuck in my mind was that we had nearly been kicked out. When I clomped up beside Cal and saw the price tag on a tiny bag of oak tree bark, I nearly had an apoplectic fit. Living in Maine meant there was no shortage of tree bark. Was my backyard a goldmine? According to Cal, I had made my exclamation a bit too loudly, and it didn't help that the salesperson was standing right behind me. Before we could be scolded by the staff, Cal turned and led me out the door onto Wharf Street. I scrutinized the map and found Wharf Street down by the waterfront. I then followed the roads in the direction we walked until I came to a recognizable landmark. I recalled facing the Hawthorne Hotel, named after the Salem born author, and turning left. According to the map this was Essex Street.

"Emma, try looking up occult shops on Essex Street," I said, excitedly.

"Okay, how about Crow Haven Corner," she said. "Does that sound like the shop?"

"No," I replied. "I remember having to walk up stone steps to that one. The shop with the amulet was on street level." My pulse was racing and I had to keep wiping my sweating palms on my cargo pants.

"Here's one," she said. "The Cauldron and Noose?"

"Oh my God, that's it!" I yelled, belatedly remembering we were in a library.

"Too much caffeine," Emma said and shrugged at the glowering woman across the room. "Are you sure it's the Cauldron and Noose?"

"Absolutely," I replied. "The name made me think of Bubble and Squeak, which is the name of that breakfast dish my mom makes with left over vegetables, and I remember looking at the sign and feeling all queasy. It stuck with me as kind of a morbid name."

"Okay, remind me not to go shopping with you and Cal," she said. "Ever."

I started giggling and felt nervous energy bubbling up to the surface. Looking over at the still frowning woman across the room I tried to clamp down on my laughter.

"Deal," I said. "So do they have a website?"

"Yeah," she said. "Here's their photo gallery. Look familiar?"

Some of the displays had changed and they now had an entire section devoted to Egyptian sun gods and scarabs, okay that's a strange coincidence, but the glass case was still in the same spot by the back wall. I clicked through more pictures in their gallery and gasped when I found a close-up photograph of the amulet.

"Gallows Amulet, private collection," I read aloud.

"Yuki, it looks just like Nera's amulet," she said. Emma was holding our copies of sketches depicting Nera's amulet. She was right. The design on the face of the amulet was the same.

"It says that the original source of the Gallows Amulet name is unknown, but a local collector added the amulet to their collection of items relating to the Salem witch trials," I said. "Though the provenance remains unknown, the Gallows Amulet has become a popular Salem attraction."

Son of a dung beetle. I was right. Not only did Nera's amulet exist, but it was only a two hour drive away. Now

71

I just needed to learn how to make a replica of the amulet and, oh yeah, break into an occult shop and steal the real thing. All before Samhain. Good thing I wore my four-leaf clover charm today. I would need all the luck I could get.

Chapter 12

Emma and I met Cal and Simon for lunch at Mr. Green Genes. Emma picked the restaurant, obviously, but the sandwiches were to die for and even the guys had to grudgingly admit the nachos grande was tasty. While the waitress was clearing away our dishes, Cal turned his gorgeous blue eyes my way.

"You okay?" he asked, watching me steadily.

I felt like I was falling into the sapphire depths of his eyes and shook my head to concentrate.

"Actually I have good news," I said, smiling.

Emma and I proceeded to tell the guys about our research into the Ulster Cycle and Nera's adventures on the night of Samhain. I explained my theory that Nera had survived the spirits of the dead by carrying an amulet made by the Sidhe, or fairies as they were better known. Emma pulled our photocopies of the amulet out of her backpack and I relayed how the sketches had looked familiar. Finally, I told them how we had tracked down the amulet, now called the Gallows Amulet, to an occult shop in Salem Massachusetts. Cal frowned when I mentioned my plan to swap the amulet for an imitation, worry lines wrinkling his brow, but he didn't say anything.

"So a bit of cloak and dagger, eh?" Simon said, making it sound like something dirty. *Leave it to Simon to get hot and bothered over breaking and entering.* "I did my share of thievery in my youth."

"Why does that not surprise me," I muttered under my breath.

"Too bad we're past the stone age," Emma said. "Bashing someone on the head to gain entry wasn't what we had in mind."

"Never doubt the magic hands," Simon said, waving the offended digits. "I have multiple skills you haven't witnessed yet." The last he said with a wink. "I haven't encountered a lock I couldn't finesse."

Emma muttered something about sticking to locks and forgetting about women when I decided to diffuse the situation. I had a lot to learn in a very short amount of time and didn't want to waste the next hour watching Simon and Emma fight.

"Can you teach me how to pick a lock?" I asked.

I could have asked Simon to go to Salem and steal the amulet for me, but what I was doing was already wrong and asking someone else to do the job on my behalf felt even worse. I guess I didn't have the makings of a criminal mastermind after all. *Too bad, I was getting good at the maniacal laugh.*

"There are a lot of things I could teach you, love, if you give me half a chance," Simon said, leering.

"Simon," Cal growled. Simon held his gaze, but was the first to look away.

"Do you have pictures of the shop?" Simon asked. "If I know what kind of lock we're dealing with, I can better answer your question." *Huh, I guess Simon could behave himself after all.*

Emma handed Simon the pictures we had printed from the Cauldron and Noose website. We only had one photo of the shop front that included the door, and that was at a bad angle for examining the lock, but the close ups of the amulet provided excellent detail of the lock on the glass case that housed the amulet.

"I could teach you how to pick this one blindfolded," Simon said. He looked like he was about to make a suggestive comment, but Cal froze him with a glare. "Right, well we could use more information about what kind of lock is on the front door, but no worries. The door looks ancient and there was no sign of security cameras or alarm system. I can get you in."

"That leaves the problem of making a replacement amulet for the swap," I said, pulling my sleeves down over my hands to hide the shaking. Simon had said he could help get me in, but that wouldn't do any good if I didn't have a replica of the amulet to leave in its place.

"Anyone know a goldsmith we could trust?" Emma asked. "No offense Yuki, but like I said before I just don't see you making a believable copy. You have mad skills when it comes to smelling dead people, but jewelry making? Not so much."

I rolled my eyes at Emma, but she did have a point. Creating the amulet would be difficult and I already had my hands full learning lock picking from Simon and helping Gavin's spirit find peace. We also had a missing boy to find. *No rest for the wicked.*

"Sorry," Cal said, running his hands through his hair. "I don't know anyone, but I can ask my parents."

"No need," Simon said, smugly. "I know a guy."

"Of course you do," Emma grumbled. "Is he trustworthy?"

"The best trust money can buy," Simon replied. "He's also fast, which is something we need to consider."

"I can withdraw from my savings account, but I probably don't have enough to cover what this guy will charge," I said.

Would he accept a payment plan? Maybe I could find a way to borrow money. I was short on funds after pitching in to have Emma's car repaired, but the amulet was important. I could always get a part-time job, though how I would work it around my bizarre paranormal life was beyond me. Too bad I didn't have a handy psychic ability, like knowing lottery numbers, rather than smelling the dead.

"No worries, love," Simon said, grinning. "Don't get your panties in a bunch. I can cover the expense."

I could tell that Calvin was torn between telling Simon to shut his mouth, he had said *panties* after all, and thanking him. He settled for shifting through all the colors of the spectrum. His tanned face was shifting back to angry red when I squeezed his hand. I reached up, on tip toes, to kiss Cal on the cheek and he turned to slant his mouth over mine. When we broke apart I continued to hold onto his hand. Cal looked much more relaxed. Good, Simon was doing me a favor and I didn't want him rewarded with a punch in the face. *Not today anyway.*

But how could Simon afford to pay my debt? He didn't work and I was unaware of any past work history. I realized that there was a lot about Simon, and his past, that I didn't know. Was he from a wealthy family, had he robbed a bank, or worked as a gigolo? Knowing Simon, the answer was probably all of the above. *Especially the gigolo bit.*

"Thanks, I'll pay you back," I said.

"Aye, love," Simon said, grinning. "You will."

Son of a dung beetle. I didn't like the sound of that. No, I didn't like the sound of that at all.

*****

Simon disappeared to make a clandestine call to his underground jeweler connection while Emma, Cal, and I decided what to do next. Cal filled us in on the lack of progress in finding clues to Sam's whereabouts. Sam's sister was frantic and the hint from Emma's spirit guide alluded to his capture. If Sam was still alive and being kept hidden underground, there was a chance that we could save him. The big question was why the killer had decided to kidnap him at all. Why not murder him when he had the chance? The thought made my stomach churn. Or maybe it was the increasing smell of burning brownies. *Don't worry Gavin, we'll catch this guy and help you find peace.*

"Why do you think this guy is keeping Sam alive?" I asked. "If he hates werewolves so much, why didn't he kill his target? I mean, I'm glad he didn't kill Sam, but it seems weird he would go to the trouble to attempt a kidnapping."

"Maybe he messed up?" Emma suggested.

"Oh God," Cal said. "This guy hates werewolves, right? The silver bullet, cross, mountain ash, mistletoe, and wolfsbane he left beneath Gavin's body were obviously wards against lycanthropy. Plus, Gavin's body was in wolf form when he died..."

"He wants to kill Sam when he's in wolf form," I guessed. I wrinkled my nose at the growing smell of burning brownies, but tried to concentrate.

"Psycho," Emma said. "What kind of werewolf goes around hunting other werewolves and killing them in their wolf form?"

"I think the real question, love, is why does our killer hate werewolves?" Simon said, sliding back into his seat. I hadn't heard him approach and wondered how much of our conversation he had heard. "If we knew the answer to that, then we might be able to figure out who he is."

"Okay, we can call around and ask if anyone knows of a pack member who was ever attacked or slighted by another werewolf," Cal said. "I've already been working on a list of known ronin or, ah, lone wolves. Maybe we can narrow our search to people who show up on both lists."

"How about adding a crazy category?" I asked. "You know Loco Lycans."

"I know who would top *that* list," Emma said, looking pointedly at Simon. *Actually, she had a point.*

"While you're all running around making lists, you may want to keep an eye on the moon," Simon said. "If this killer wants our boy in wolf form before he kills him, then he'll be getting his wish soon enough." Simon turned to me and winked. "See kitten, you're not the only one on a tight schedule. Lady Moon will be full two nights after Samhain."

"Not good," Emma muttered.

When we all looked at her quizzically she pulled her cell phone from her purse. After bringing up a calendar, she showed us the notation for November first. *Son of a dung beetle.* November first was also known as the Day of the Dead. It looked like we would be facing a full moon and some full on spirit activity after Samhain. I had been so focused on the events of Samhain night that I had completely overlooked the threats of the days after. Our spirit storm had just upgraded to a spirit hurricane. Oh well, at least now it didn't look like things could get much worse.

"Yuki, you better hope those witches don't figure out who stole their amulet, 'cause you're going to need all your mojo for this whole Day of the Dead thing," Emma said.

Oh yeah, cursed by witches. *Note to self, things can always get worse.*

Chapter 13

After lunch Emma left for her shift at the shelter and Cal, Simon, and I went back to the cabin which was doubling as command central. We each stuffed our pockets with food, beef jerky for the guys and granola bars for me, and water. I was glad to be wearing my paratrooper cargo pants since they had a gazillion pockets. My pants were tucked into my boots, leaving nothing to snag on rocks or debris. Scanning our supplies I also grabbed two flashlights. It couldn't hurt to have a back up. I also put one in a plastic bag to keep it dry. I really didn't want to end up underground without a working flashlight. The guys, and the other searchers, had their heightened werewolf eyesight, but I was only human and all too afraid of the dark, especially when a killer may be lurking in the shadows. *On second thought, maybe I should grab another flashlight.*

Cal had spread a map on the table and was staring at it intensely. I could see the tension in his shoulders and the dark circles beneath his eyes. His hands fisted and unclasped compulsively as he looked at the map for answers. He was the alpha and, therefore, responsible for protecting his pack. Losing one pack member to a brutal killer had forced Cal to take on his leadership role early. He hadn't fully come into his powers, and still struggled with controlling his wolf spirit, but he didn't shirk his responsibilities. Watching him worry over Sam, I suddenly fell in love with him even more. I didn't even know that was possible. *You're full of surprises Calvin Miller.*

I moved to his side, hips touching, and examined the map. From this vantage I could see hundreds of small marks where Cal had checked off areas searched. It looked like they had begun searching near Sam's home and then radiated outward. It was impressive how much ground they had covered, but so far it hadn't been enough. I let my gaze roam further out from the center and looked for anywhere that may house a fugitive underground.

A memory of being in a cave with Cal was nagging at me, but I couldn't place where exactly the cave had been. We had only been about ten years old at the time so it couldn't have been very far away.

"Cal, remember when you read that book on vision quests and we went looking for the perfect meditation cave?" I asked. "Your book made it sound wonderful and peaceful, but what they didn't mention was it being dark, wet, and scary as Hell." I shuddered at the memory. "I recall what it was like being inside the cave, probably scarred for life with that memory, but I can't remember where it was. Can you?"

"Wow, I had totally forgotten about that day," Cal said. "Hey, you broke all the rules."

"Silly rules," I said a little defensively. "Plus, you were the one that agreed to darkness, isolation, and fasting. Not me. I was just there for moral support and to run for help if you broke an ankle or something."

Simon, who had been sitting quietly, started laughing. "You brought a girl into a dark cave, alone, and you purposefully ignored her and tried to meditate?" he said.

"Ignore him," I said, rolling my eyes at Simon. "We need to figure out where those caves were."

"I know just how to find out," Cal said happily.

Cal ran to his parent's house and returned with his old book on vision quests. While he was gone I studiously checked my pockets and ignored Simon. *Fortunately I had a lot of pockets.*

"See," Cal said, opening the book and setting it on the table. "There was a section for documenting your vision quest, but since someone distracted me from my meditation I ended up doodling a map to the cave."

"Is that a pond?" I asked, pointing at a circular lumpy thing.

"No, that's the cave," Cal said.

"Is this a river?" Simon asked, pointing at a squiggly line.

"No, that's the road, Cal said, sighing. "I guess I'll be the one to read the map, since obviously no one else can make heads or tails of it."

Simon and I looked at each other and laughed. Cal's childhood artistic skills left a lot to be desired, but I didn't doubt he could lead us to the cave. Just a walk along the squiggle and we'd be at the lumpy bump, aka the cave, where Sam may be waiting for us. *I guess we were going spelunking.*

Cal grabbed a first aid kit and stuffed more items into the pockets of his hoodie. He was wearing low slung jeans that tugged even lower when he attached a coil of rope to his belt loop with a metal carabiner. I lost all ability to breathe as he reached into one of the overhead cabinets for a lighter. A few inches of tanned skin were peeking below his shirt and a curve of hip bone showing. He was, in a word, hot and I couldn't help but notice.

Feeling my face turn bright red, I turned away and walked into Simon who chuckled. "Ready?" he asked.

My suddenly sluggish brain could not compute. *Huh?* Oh yeah, the cave. "Sure, I have everything I need," I said, trying not to sound flustered.

"Are you sure you want to go with us?" Cal asked, looking at me steadily. *I hope I'm not still blushing.* "You could stay here and wait for our call."

My head suddenly filled with the pungent smell of burning brownies. "No way," I said. "I'm definitely going this time. I think I can use the strength of Gavin's smell impression as a guide. If the smell gets stronger, then chances are we're heading in the right direction."

"We can certainly use your mad skills," Cal said, moving closer, cupping my face and brushing his thumb along my jaw line. He kissed my temple then reached for the door.

"She also has every sodding flashlight we own," Simon grumbled.

*****

When we reached the cave I stopped to send a text message to Emma with our coordinates. I wasn't stupid. I've watched all of the horror movies and suspense thrillers. This is the part when the music gets ominous and you want to shout, "Don't go in there!" because you figure no one knows where the characters are heading and their cell phones probably won't get a signal underground. I figured by letting Emma know exactly where we would be, I was changing our luck. *A little reverse psychology on Fate can't hurt, right?*

I reluctantly handed one of my flashlights to Simon who immediately clicked it on. I guess werewolves don't have perfect vision in the dark after all. Cal reached for a small flashlight he had stashed in his hoodie pocket and I turned one of my lights to the cave mouth. All three lights barely illuminated the inky blackness of the cave.

The opening was just large enough for Cal to walk upright. We could have brushed the sides of the cave walls with our fingertips if we extended our arms. I tried to fight down a feeling of claustrophobia. The increasing burnt brownie smell was making the small dark space feel all the more confining and I struggled to use my yoga breathing to stay calm.

"Sense anything?" Cal asked in a whisper.

"The smell impression seems stronger here," I said, keeping my voice low. "I think we're in the right place."

"Aye, my wolf feels it too," Simon said in a low growl. "The killer has been here."

My heart sped up at the thought of sharing the darkness with a murderer and I felt a bead of perspiration slide down my spine.

"In Stygian cave forlorn," I whispered.

"Milton," Simon said, with what seemed begrudging respect. "A fitting passage. L'Allegro?"

"Yes," I said, nodding and feeling gooseflesh on my neck. "Hence, loathèd Melancholy, Of Cerberus and blackest Midnight born, In Stygian cave forlorn, 'Mongst horrid shapes, and shrieks, and sights unholy."

"Could you two not quote the creepiest lines ever?" Cal asked. "I just felt like someone was walking over my grave."

"No talk of graves," I said lightly.

"We can talk of shrieks and sights unholy, but not of graves," Cal said. "Got it, my bad."

I gave Cal a light punch on the shoulder and I could have sworn Simon rolled his eyes.

"Okay children, no time for stalling," Simon said, loping forward.

Cal and I walked hand in hand with Simon in the lead. We kept our flashlights low to prevent stumbling over fallen rocks. A few times Simon got down on all fours to search the ground, one time even tasting the dirt, but he always conferred with us regarding my smell impressions before deciding on a direction to take. The deeper into the cave we went the more tunnels we found branching off. More than once Simon scouted ahead only to find dead ends.

As we turned down a new tunnel Simon raised his hand for us to stop. The smell of burning brownies nearly knocked me over. Cal squeezed my hand and cocked his head to the side as though listening for something. Simon too seemed to be listening intently, but motioned for us to proceed slowly. Inching forward I began to hear a faint thumping. Just as I was about to ask the others if they heard it too, Cal turned and whispered in my ear.

"If you quote the Tell-Tale heart, I may shriek like a girl," Cal whispered softly.

Now that he mentioned it the sound did resemble a heartbeat. *Great, like this place wasn't spooky enough.*

Cal squeezed my hand and we continued forward. When we rounded the next bend in the tunnel Simon rushed forward to a heap of clothing on the floor. But that wasn't exactly right. The pile of rags was the source of the pounding sound. *Oh God, had we found Sam?*

Assaulted by burnt brownie smell, I hesitated before entering the larger space, but Cal, in his eagerness, led us forward.

"He's alive!" Simon exclaimed, turning to us with relief in his eyes, but his face quickly turned to horror followed by rage.

Suddenly the hand that Cal held was left outstretched, naked in the cold emptiness of his absence. Cal was tumbling on the floor, someone, or something, on his back. The cave echoed with their growls and the light of my flashlight streaked over their bodies as they rolled and clawed with inhuman speed. Startled by Simon's wolf form as he joined the melee, I watched seconds, that felt like hours, pass in the still frame flashes of a child's flipbook.

The snarls and growls were being steadily replaced by the roaring in my ears. *Probably going into shock*, part of my mind worried, but there was no room for concern for myself. My entire universe consisted of flashes of Cal, my soul mate, struggling to fight a deranged killer. I could reach out and touch him if they would only stop moving with such deadly swiftness.

For a frozen moment Cal was flying through the air, his body thrown, and the roaring in my ears was replaced with a sickening crack as his head hit an outcropping of stone. *No. Please no.*

Running to Cal's side I touched his face with a shaking hand. Cal's eyelids fluttered briefly at my touch, but he lay where he fell, his head against a large rock. A line of blood was running down over his right eyebrow to pool in the crease of his eye before traveling over his cheek to drip from his chin. I didn't look behind me at the continuing fight, but I wondered who, or what, could be making that horrible shrieking wail. *Oh, that would be me.*

Tearing my gaze from Cal's unconscious face, I scanned the room desperately looking for some way to help him. A blur of movement caught my eye and I watched as Simon grabbed his assailant's hand in his sharp toothed mouth. With an explosion of fur his opponent shifted to wolf form. The man's transformation left him momentarily vulnerable and Simon pressed his advantage. Simon pounced onto the wolf's back, gripping its neck between his teeth.

A small smoldering voice inside me was glad to see the monster who had injured Cal, and murdered and kidnapped members of his pack, receive retribution, but my heart knew how very wrong that voice was. When Simon and I locked eyes, I shook my head no. I still wasn't able to speak, but my message was clear. Another death wouldn't make this situation any better. In slow motion, I removed the coil of rope from Cal's belt loop and carried it to where Simon was holding the wolf. I tied his forelegs and hind legs with numb fingers, then stepped away as Simon shifted to human form. Taking a piece of shredded clothing he tied a muzzle around the wolf's snout.

Shredded clothing? *Oh yeah.* Simon had transformed mid-battle shredding his clothes as he shifted into wolf form. I pulled off my hoodie, tossing it to him, and looked around for something more helpful. My hoodie would be really, really short on him. I limped over to the pile of clothes in the corner, but jumped back when it groaned. *Son of a dung beetle.* I had forgotten all about Sam during the attack. He seemed to be buried beneath a pile of clothing, so I grabbed a pair of shorts and tossed them behind myself. *Hopefully Simon puts them on.*

Pulling away more of the clothing I could see Sam's frightened face. He was staring straight ahead with sightless eyes, groaning, and pounding on the stone floor. That must have been the thumping sound we heard before. Sam was in shock, or worse, and didn't respond when I whispered his name. I left a bottle of water near his hand and dragged myself back over to Calvin.

Blood from Cal's head had run down to soak his shirt and I belatedly remembered the first aid supplies he had shoved in his hoodie pockets back at the cabin. I carefully reached into his pockets, hands shaking, and found a bag filled with gauze pads and an ace bandage. I pulled a pack of tissues from one of my pants pockets and gently wiped away the blood on his face and head. There was already a large bump forming with a cut in the center. There was a lot of blood, but the cut didn't look as bad as the bump. Peeling off the wrapper, I placed two gauze pads on the gash and wound the bandage around his head to keep it in place. I whimpered in frustration when I realized I didn't have a way to fasten the bandage, but just as I was about to break into sobs I saw dim light shine on the safety pins I had attached to my arm warmers. I would have laughed about MacGyvering the bandage, but this was no time for laughter. *I may never laugh again.*

Cal's face looked so pale. Think Yuki, think. I needed to call Emma. She could bring her medical supplies. Emma would know what to do.

"How is he?" Simon asked as he knelt beside me. He was wearing the shorts, but not my hoodie.

At least he's wearing something. "He...he hit his head," I said, my voice raspy. How long had I been screaming? "I thought I heard something...crack when he hit the rocks. There's a cut and a nasty bump. I wrapped it with gauze, but he lost a lot of blood." My voice quivered as I said "blood" and I closed my eyes. I could feel my lips shake as I drew in a calming breath. "Sam looks like he's in shock," I said. It was easier to talk about a stranger. "I left him a bottle of water, but he just sits there staring into space and pounding the floor. I...I can't imagine what he's been through."

"It's all right," Simon said, soothingly. "Everything will be all right. We heal faster than humans, so don't worry about that scrape. I'm more worried about the bump, but I'm sure he'll be fine with some rest. Sam too. Were you hurt?"

Simon looked at me intently and I realized I was covered in blood. Not my blood, Cal's blood.

"I'm okay," I answered. "None of it is mine," I said, gesturing to the blood. "I was just about to call Emma."

"Good," Simon said, nodding. "Tell her to bring a stretcher if she can get her hands on one. A backboard with neck support would be even better, but she needs to get here fast. I'll meet her at the mouth of the cave."

Great, that leaves me alone in the dark with a trussed up murderer, an incoherent boy in shock, and Cal. *Cal who won't wake up.*

Emma will know what to do. Maybe she has a tea that cures head wounds. I speed dialed Emma and prayed that Cal would be okay.

*****

Emma arrived in record time. Or maybe it just seemed that way. Everything was a blur. She assessed Cal's wounds first, and with Simon's assistance, secured him to a backboard. They wrapped a foam cervical collar around his neck and Emma placed a poultice on his head wound. She explained why, swelling or something, but my mind wouldn't focus. I kept replaying the sound of Cal's head cracking as it hit hard stone. I may have teased Cal about having a thick skull, but now I hoped that it was true. Peeling his eyelids back, Emma used my flashlight to check his pupils' response to light. After checking Cal's vitals one more time she turned her attention to Sam.

Sam remained huddled beneath a pile of discarded rags by the wall. He gazed into space, still rocking back and forth, but had stopped pounding the floor. Simon guessed that Sam had been trying to call for help. When his voice became hoarse from screaming he had turned to slapping the stone floor. Help had arrived, but Sam's terror was far from gone. He appeared to be living in his own personal Hell. A place I longed to send his captor.

Emma barely spared a glance at the murderer trussed on the floor. She would normally do anything to help any living creature, but this werewolf was a killer. He had been stalking Cal's pack and had already tasted blood once. Emma didn't show her usual gentleness or kindness as she completed a cursory examination of his wounds. "He'll live," she spat, making it sound like a curse.

Emma directed Simon in the evacuation of the cave. I stayed wherever Cal lay, never letting go of his hand. When Emma pulled her mom's van into my driveway I just blinked in confusion. What were we doing here? *When did we get into the van?*

"You have to let go now, love," Simon said gently, as he pried my fingers from Cal's hand. "Time to get you home to your parents."

I gripped Cal's hand more tightly and stared mutely at Simon.

"Yuki, it's okay," Emma said. "I'm pretty sure that Cal has a concussion. We need to get him back to the cabin, but you need to go home. The pack can't have your parents getting curious." I loosened my grip and let her slide her cool hand into mine. "You need sleep. Let me get you inside."

Emma led me inside and up to my room. Once I was in bed she clicked the overhead light off and turned to leave.

"What about Cal?" I asked, staring at the ceiling.

"He'll be okay," Emma said. "I promise." Then she was gone.

I couldn't lose Cal. The pain of potential loss was all consuming, like stepping into a shadow and being swallowed whole, leaving nothing but darkness.

Chapter 14

The sound of wind rustling through tall grass made me open my eyes. *Since when did grass grow in my bedroom?* Gazing up at the ashen sky I could see blades of grass waving beside me. Pulling myself into a sitting position I looked at my surroundings. I appeared to be in a large field. Seeing no apparent threats, I stood. Where I had lain grew a small patch of beautiful blossoming wild flowers. *Strange I didn't crush them.* That wasn't the only thing that was odd about this place. Turning a pirouette, on the ball of my booted foot, I could see only grass in every direction.

Reaching down to touch the soil, I sent out a questioning thought to my spirit guide. "Why am I here?" I asked, silently.

I had discovered my assigned spirit animal at Shaman Camp with Cal. His kind of fun, not mine. Shaman Camp involved way too much dirt and hand holding and not nearly enough bathing. I stayed long enough to participate in a special ceremony where I was informed that my spirit animal was the scarab, or dung beetle. Not something I was overly excited about. Cal's spirit animal, of course, was the wolf.

In previous dreams I had been able to manifest either my scarab spirit guide or Cal's wolf spirit. Scarabs have a connection to the earth, hence touching the soil, but my spirit guide had said to return to her when I had learned "to walk the world of dreams and darkness." I wasn't so sure that I had learned enough in the past few weeks to warrant her help.

Digging my fingers into the moist soil I closed my eyes and I asked my question again. "Why am I here?" I asked.

A tingling began in my fingers and ran up through my arms. A warm pulsing rose up through my feet and I knew in which direction to walk. Good thing, since everything in this place looked the same. Striding forward I was shocked to see flowers blossoming wherever I stepped. Staring at the flowers rising up around my boots, I nearly fell when I heard a familiar voice.

"You always were so full of life," Cal said.

Cal. "Oh God, you're here!" I exclaimed, launching myself into his arms. "I was so worried." Closing my eyes, I drank in his smell and the feel of him encircling me.

"Yuki, open your eyes," he said.

Gazing up at Cal's handsome face I etched every detail into memory. I vowed to never again be apart from his shaggy hair that fell into deep blue eyes and the full mouth that I now longed to kiss.

I had recently promised myself that I would never let him get hurt again, but he did get hurt. I had been the catalyst when he lost control of his human form at the Homecoming dance and I had stood helpless as he was attacked earlier this evening. I needed to become stronger. I needed to train with the pack and learn how to help protect those I loved, protect Cal, and not be a liability. *I love you so much Calvin Miller.*

"Look at where we touch," Cal said, his voice sad.

Curious, I looked at where his arms encircled my own. Though he felt solid, I had sunk an inch or more into him. He was fading, still substantial at the center, but transparent along his skin. Was he a ghost? *Was he...dead?*

"I don't...Cal, I don't understand," I said, brushing my left hand through his arm. He felt warm, but he was not as solid as I originally thought. But I could still feel the heat of him. He can't be dead. *He just can't.*

"I...I think I'm dying," he said, voice quavering. "I keep losing my wolf spirit and...I believe I may die if I can't be reunited with him."

"God Cal, don't say that," I said. "I can't lose you. I just can't."

"We won't ever lose each other," Cal said, stroking my cheek. "Remember, no matter what happens, you're my soul mate. You complete me."

"What can I do to help?" I asked, trying to remain hopeful. *I won't let you leave me Calvin Miller.*

"When you leave this place, I need you to call my wolf spirit," Cal said, intently. "Each time I've seen him here he has been standing on a fallen log reaching towards a glowing light. Yuki, we can't let him go into the light. I think if that were to happen I would die. I need my wolf spirit in order to live."

"Can't we just find him again?" I asked. "What if you talk to him?"

"I can't get close to him," Cal said, shaking his head. "When I try to, he disappears. I haven't even been able to find the log he stands on. Yuki, I need your help. Can you dance for me?"

"Yes," I said. "I'll call your wolf spirit back to you. I promise."

"Thank you," Cal whispered, pulling me closer to him. I tried not to notice how I drifted through him. "Oh no."

I opened my eyes and followed Cal's gaze to the ground. The flowers by my feet were shriveling and turning black.

"Yuki, you have to go," Cal said.

"I don't want to leave you," I said, shakily.

"This place will draw the life from you," Cal said. "You're fully alive. You don't belong here. You have to go now."

"I love you," I said, looking up into his eyes.

"I love you more," Cal said, kissing my cheek and then my lips. "Now run. Run and don't look back."

I ran. Tears streaming down my face, gasping for breath, I ran as fast and as far as my legs would take me. I ran away from the man I loved, hurtling towards my destiny.

Chapter 15

I awoke gasping and churning the covers with my legs. I had made it home, safely back in my body for now, and needed to find Cal. Sitting up in bed I felt pressure building behind my eyes and pain at my temples. Great, a migraine was not something I needed today. Unfortunately the only thing that helped my headaches was a dose of Emma's horrific tasting tea. I guess I would just have to drink her noxious brew and wash it down with the bitter truth. Cal was hovering on the brink of death and I was the only person with a chance to save him. *No pressure or anything.*

Hands shaking, I hastily dressed and brushed my teeth. My eyes were puffy from last night's crying and surrounded by dark circles. I grabbed a pair of sunglasses from the pile of accessories on my vanity and slid them on. *Better.*

I didn't want my parents asking questions about my ragged appearance. It wasn't like I could be truthful about Cal's condition. If Cal couldn't seek medical attention at a hospital, then his concussion would have to remain a secret from those outside the pack. My mom loved Calvin and there was no way she would understand him lying at home in a coma. She may respect his parents' wishes to a point, but my mom wasn't the kind of woman to stand by and watch while someone she cared about was hurt. If there was something she could do, then she would risk a great deal to help, a passing friendship with his parents be damned. It was funny, but in that way my mom and I were a lot alike. *Guess I know where I get it from.*

Walking down the stairs and into the kitchen, I attempted to act normal. Reaching for the coffee pot, I filled a travel mug and carefully twisted on the lid. My dad looked up when I pulled my backpack over my shoulder and headed toward the door.

"Leaving so soon?" he asked, smiling. He was sitting at the table looking over the Sunday paper, his scuffed slippers propped on a nearby chair.

I made a mental note to buy him a new pair of slippers for Christmas. *If I'm still around then.* The thought crept in and shattered the moment.

"Sorry Dad, Emma and I have plans to go apple picking," I said. My parents worked all week and I felt guilty rushing off the one day they were home, but Cal needed me.

"Have fun," he said, attention swinging back to his newspaper.

I was glad that it had been my dad, not my mom, in the kitchen. She was way more perceptive and a pair of sunglasses probably wouldn't have been enough to hide the truth. Thank goodness for small favors. With one last glance, I turned and walked out into a cold new day.

*****

Huddled against the cold, I walked quickly. I could have called Emma for a ride, but knew she probably had been up all night tending to Cal and Sam. She may even have provided medical care to our murderer. My hands involuntarily tightened into fists. Just thinking about the man who attacked Cal, putting him into a coma, made my blood boil. Maybe the cool air would help clear my head.

I breathed deeply, filling my nose with the sickly sweet smell of rotten crab apples. My long black skirt swish swished as I waded through the sea of fallen leaves. The familiar sounds and smells were calming, and for the first time I realized that the smell of burnt brownies was gone.

We caught Gavin's killer. Perhaps that was all he needed for his soul to find peace.

I had recently been told that I was the light that helped lead lost souls out of darkness. Helping the spirits of the dead was a task I took seriously, but this morning I didn't feel like celebrating. I was glad that Gavin had found peace, but I wasn't feeling like a wondrous beacon of light. *More like a storm cloud filled with unshed tears.*

I was having a hard time dealing with what had happened last night. Calvin wasn't just my soul mate. He was my best friend. I couldn't imagine a world that didn't include Cal, and didn't want to. How could one madman come into our lives and cause so much pain? This was one storm cloud who wouldn't mind striking that man down. *Maybe if I'm angry enough lightning bolts will shoot out my butt.* I continued down the leaf strewn sidewalk, tears of frustration rolling down my face to fall on my black blouse. Diamonds of pain left to sparkle in the morning sun.

Eventually the cabin came within sight and I realized that I had been walking in a daze. *Calvin is in there and he needs my help.* Heart hammering in my chest, I quickened my pace and strode up the path to the door. With a rap on the door frame, I ducked inside. The only light was the dust mote filled sunbeams streaming in through the cabin windows. Moving aside to shut the door, I stepped into the room, catching my foot on something large and soft, and fell across one warm body to land, spread eagle, on a second. Guess I should have turned on the lights. *So much for trying not to wake everyone up.*

"Well now, if you wanted to get inside my sleeping bag," Simon quipped, "all you had to do was ask. Of course, I'm not complaining, love. Waking up with a girl on top of me isn't a bad way to start my morning, but I could have done without the elbow in the ribs."

It was too dark to tell, but I was sure he just winked at me. Pushing away from Simon, and giving an extra jab with my elbow, I heard a mumbled yelp.

"Yuki, watch where you stick that thing," Emma grumbled.

Wincing, I looked behind me to see my booted left foot an inch from Emma's mouth. "Sorry!" I exclaimed, disentangling myself from their sleeping bags. "What are you guys doing anyway?"

"I can't speak for wolf man over there, but I was trying to get some sleep," Emma said sulkily.

"In front of the door?" I asked.

"It was either that or sleep next to Simon," Emma said. "Since Hell hasn't frozen over yet, I slept in front of the door."

"If you guys had to sleep on the floor, then...?" I began to ask.

"Yeah, yeah loverboy is sleeping soundly on the bed," Simon finished for me.

I stumbled over to the corner where Cal lay unmoving on the bed. Someone, probably Emma, had pulled the soft quilt up over his arms and shoulders to sit just beneath his chin. Beneath the blankets he was positioned on his back with arms at his sides. Corpse Pose my mind volunteered. With a shudder I pulled one of his arms out from under the blankets and held his hand.

It felt strange holding him without being held in return. No hello squeeze, or comforting embrace, just a limp hand to trace with my fingers. I turned his hand over and looked at the network of intersecting lines and grooves. A few years ago Cal had dared me into going with him to a palm reader. A "chiromancy" appointment he called it. When we arrived I was surprised to see that the woman who would read our fortunes was a blond woman in her forties, not the dark haired crone I had envisioned. She had looked at Cal strangely at first, but then nodded her head and told him happily that he had a strong life line. Cal had believed her, but she could have been a charlatan. I suddenly hoped that her reading had been accurate. I needed Cal to keep on living. I couldn't lose him now.

"Earth to Yuki," Emma said, sitting on the chair beside me.

I wondered how long she had been sitting there. "Sorry," I said, trying, and failing, to look away from Cal.

"Dude you need to get some sleep," Emma said, frowning.

"No, I slept," I said. "That's actually part of why I'm here."

I told Emma and Simon about my dream and how Cal had described being separated from his wolf spirit.

"You were right," Emma said, looking worriedly at Simon.

Huh? I looked confusedly back and forth between them. I was missing something here.

"I wish I were wrong," Simon said, running his fingers through his hair with a sigh. "Last night, when we returned from the cave, I noticed the absence of Cal's wolf smell. He just smells...human."

"We can't let Cal's wolf spirit go into the light," I said, firmly. "You both agree that he could die without his wolf spirit, right?"

Emma and Simon both nodded in agreement.

"Even if I wasn't already worried about him losing a part of himself," Emma said. "I would want Cal's wolf traits strong right now. His werewolf ability to heal more rapidly than a human could be the difference between whether or not he makes it through this safely. I'm working without real medical equipment. Cal needs all the help he can get."

"Aye, I've never heard of one of us losing our wolf spirit, but it doesn't sound good," Simon said. "I know that I couldn't live without mine. We are both a part of each other."

"Then it's settled," I said. "I am going to dance to call Cal's wolf spirit back to his body. If I can communicate with his wolf, then I'll try to explain how important it is for it to stay here with Cal."

"What do you need?" Emma asked.

"Let's roll up these sleeping bags and clear the floor," I said. "And Emma?"

"Yeah?" Emma asked.

"Do you have any of your headache ease tea with you?" I said, wincing.

"Sure thing," she said. "It's out in the van."

Emma grabbed her keys and ran out to get her herbal supplies. I turned to see Simon staring at me intently. Raising one eyebrow he said, "You must really love Cal if you're willing to drink Emma's tea to help him."

"Yeah, I really do," I said, walking over to look down at Cal's sleeping face. *I really, really do.*

Chapter 16

Emma and Simon sat against the far wall, each with a drum and stick. Cal had acquired the drums last year at Shaman Camp. They were hoop drums he had made by hand, stretching wet rawhide across the wooden hoop making a taught skin on one side for drumming and leaving the exposed strands on the back for holding the drum. The rawhide strands could also be pulled and released to alter the tone of the drum when hit by the stick. The drumming sticks were covered on one end with some kind of padding and more rawhide.

As Emma and Simon began to pound a slow beat on their drums, I stepped into the center of the room. I clapped my hands and stomped my feet to the beat of the drums and began to walk in a circle. Step, stomp-clap, step, stomp-clap. As the drumming became faster I increased my pace and began swaying as I circled the room. I visualized Cal's wolf loping towards me. I tried to concentrate and focus on that image, but it was harder than ever before. Sweat beaded on my forehead and I struggled to suck enough air into my lungs. I continued dancing, stomping and writhing with impromptu dance movements, always maintaining my circle.

I reached my arms out, grasping for Cal's wolf spirit, but my hands moved only through air. *Come to us. Calvin needs you.* His wolf should have been running to us by now, but I hadn't felt even the tiniest spark of its presence. Over the sound of drumming I heard the unmistakable sound of a wolf howling. For a moment I thought it was Cal's wolf, but realized it was only Simon adding his own beckoning call. I imagined running my hands over Cal's wolf and sinking my hands into its fur. Dancing crazily I pictured myself embracing his wolf and nuzzling his neck where I could catch his scent.

Feeling an electric charge in the air I realized that I *could* smell Cal's wolf. The smell was faint, but it meant that our call had reached him. My dancing, and Emma and Simon's drumming, became faster and faster and I could feel Cal's wolf spirit moving toward us. It moved with painful slowness, but eventually I could feel the weight of its stare. *Please, help Cal. He needs you. Without you he may die. Please stay here with him.*

I remember one more turn around the circle then slipping to the floor as everything faded to black...

*****

Dirt skittered by my head and I blinked dust from my eyes. *Where was I?* My question was answered as a large insectoid head came into view. Pushing myself into a sitting position I could see that the head was connected to an enormous black shelled body.

Clubbed antennae began waving in the air as she scented the air around me. I had researched a bit about dung beetles, aka scarabs, in recent months and had learned they had an amazing sense of smell. It was strange having something in common with a towering beetle, but I suppose she was my spirit guide for a reason.

"You have been busy child," she said.

I know beetles can't really speak, but, as before, she communicated her words directly into my mind.

"Busy, busy that's me," I said. *Think Yuki, think. Maybe she can help you with Cal's wolf spirit.*

"The spirits of the dead surround you," the beetle's voice whispered in my head. "Their scent is all around you child."

"Uh, yeah about that," I said. "Cal was injured and his wolf spirit is trying to leave him, to go into the light, but if that happens Cal will die. Cal told me once that I could be his anchor to the human world, but I don't know how

100

to hold his wolf spirit. Do you know how I can keep his wolf spirit from walking into the light?"

"I may know a way little one, but you must first make a promise," she said. "Heed these words, child. Let the spirits guide you, but never let them take you."

"What do you mean by, never let them take me?" I asked. There was something foreboding about her pronouncement and I suddenly wondered if this was why there weren't many others like me. *Maybe some of us reach out to the spirits as they head into the light...and never come back.*

"The spirits of the dead are lost, flotsam in the darkness of the in-between worlds, grasping for the way home," she said. "You, child, are one of the few who can sense the clues that help resolve their unfinished business and lead them to the light, but you must be careful. You are the candle flame in the darkness that the dead may follow, but have you never wondered where that light comes from? You share a spark of the light from beyond and like calls to like. The pull of the light can be strong little one, especially when the spirit you seek is a part of one you love."

"Okay, I promise not to follow the spirits of the dead into the light," I said. "How can I save Cal?"

"Renew your ties, little one," she said. "Find the spirit-ink man and do what your young man has done before you. But beware that when the ink slips beneath your skin you will be bound to him more strongly."

"I don't mind being bound to Calvin," I said. "He's my soul mate." *My one true love.*

"The stronger you are bound to him the more difficult it will be to resist the pull of the light," she said. "You must consider the risk to your soul. If you do as I say and still cannot hold his wolf spirit, then you may face your own death."

"Cal is worth the risk," I said. *I will not lose you Calvin Miller.*

"You do not have much time," she said. "The storm is fast approaching and you must be prepared."

"What do you mean?" I asked.

"Have you forgotten child?" she asked. "The veil begins to thin. Samhain is nigh upon us and you, little one, are in grave danger."

"Right now, I don't really care about that," I said.

"Oh you should care, little one," the beetle said. "Death is not the worst this spirit horde is capable of. Try to help your love, but prepare for the storm."

Chapter 17

I bolted awake to the crack of thunder. The drumming of rain on the roof seemed unusually loud and I realized I wasn't home in my bedroom. As my eyes focused I saw the outline of raw timbers and beside me I watched the hypnotic rise and fall of Cal's chest as he slept. *Oh right, I was in the cabin, but had my dancing helped Cal or was he still in a coma?*

"Nice of you to finally join us," Simon said from the kitchen.

I looked up to see Emma and Simon sitting with steaming mugs at the small counter.

"Please tell me that's coffee," I groaned. I felt like my mouth was filled with sand. *Maybe it was.*

"It's tea, but don't worry, I have black tea, not just the herbal kind," Emma said.

Thank all that's holy. I would have preferred coffee, but black tea with lots of sugar could give me the jolt I needed just as well. "How's Cal?" I asked. "Did we help? Any improvement?" I stood up with a lurch and headed to the kitchen counter.

"Slow down zombie girl," Emma said. "Have you looked at yourself? You danced your butt off and passed out. You're so pale even a ghost would be scared. Come sit while I make you some tea."

I turned to Simon and tried, and failed, to raise one eyebrow questioningly. He seemed to get the message though. Who knew he'd be the reasonable one? Maybe while I slept aliens came and switched their brains. Stranger things have happened. *I should know.*

"Cal's vitals are stronger now, love, so yes I think your dance helped," Simon answered. He even seemed to be giving me most of the credit. *Oh yeah, aliens definitely switched their brains while I was out.*

"He's right," Emma said, shrugging. "Cal's temperature and blood pressure are back to normal and he seems stable, but I'm sorry hun, he hasn't woken up yet."

"That's okay," I said, with a gleam in my eye. "I know what I have to do."

"What are you planning to do?" Emma asked. She looked worried. *I must really look as bad as she said.*

"I need to see a man about a tattoo," I said.

*****

After Emma got over the initial shock, and I had slugged down a half dozen mugs of tea, we started working on a plan. According to Simon this spirit-ink dude wasn't easy to come by. He was often away in reclusive meditation and there was a ritual that had to be performed in order to get the tattoo. *How did I know this wasn't going to be easy?*

Simon "put out feelers" in the wolf community and, for now, we had to sit back and wait. Have you ever had to sit at the sickbed of someone you love? Idly sitting there, watching their chest rise and fall with the incessant ticking of the clock, is one of the most helpless feelings and I had already done this once this month. Granted the first time wasn't nearly as serious, but if I could do something to turn back time and prevent all of Cal's injuries I would. With inactivity came thoughts of who had done this to Cal and the old anger began to creep in. The red hot anger reached my heart and turned to fiery rage. It took all of the control that Simon had recently taught me, and the yoga breathing exercises I had learned while attending classes with Cal, to grab hold of that burning ember and extinguish it. Anger would only help our enemies and Cal would never forgive me if I lost myself to revenge.

I could almost hear Cal's voice chiding me and reminding me of his favorite philosophy, ahimsha. Ahimsha, or devanagari in Sanskrit, meant to do no harm. Cal had always been drawn to Eastern philosophies and I remember the day he excitedly told me about ahimsha. This philosophy was not just a declaration of nonviolence, it was a way of viewing the world. Cal was always like that, eager to find beauty in all things. *Like how he found beauty in me.*

No, I wouldn't succumb to the rage inside of me. Wasn't that the road to madness? In fact, it was probably what led to all of this pain in the first place. Simon, when asked, had told me that the man who committed these crimes had been driven mad when he was abandoned at the time of his wolf awakening. The man's ravings had been corroborated with what others could add to his story. His father had died when he was just a boy and when he was a teen his mother left him for a man. *How alone must he have felt? How scared?*

With no one to explain to him the changes in his body, he must have been frightened out of his mind. Apparently he became so paranoid of discovery that he withdrew from the human world entirely. With no school and no job he drifted, always keeping to the shadows. Living on the waste of human society, making his home in sewers and caves, he became more feral. He also became more and more convinced that his mother had left him because of his wolf side, the part of him that he relied on more each day to survive. The paradox of his self loathing and need for survival fed his madness and his desire to seek revenge on others of his kind. He became a werewolf killer.

I think I understood Cal's attraction to ahimsha. The more I thought of the killer, whose name I learned was Nathan, the sorrier I felt for him. Circumstances had left him a homeless teen with no family. His wolf transformations were confusing and terrifying, making him too afraid to turn to anyone for help. *How could I stay mad at a little lost boy who was scared and all alone?*

So instead of plotting revenge I traced the lines of Cal's tattoo with my fingertips hoping that we would soon get a call from the spirit-ink man. The tattoo was a black tribal armband, an infinity design of a wolf chasing a scarab beetle. His spirit chasing my spirit which, since they danced together in a circle, one leading to the next, meant my spirit was also chasing his. Like now. Pressing my hand against his warm decorated skin, I said a silent prayer that my spirit guide would be right. *Please let this work.*

I was so absorbed in my own little cloud of misery that I hadn't even realized Emma had left until I heard her return. Pushing through the cabin door with her arms loaded with groceries she headed to the kitchen.

"A little help here?" Emma asked, pushing shopping bags at Simon. They were the reusable tote bags, of course. Emma would never kill a tree or contribute to global warming by using paper or plastic. *Ever.*

Simon just rolled his eyes and grudgingly accepted the bags as Emma turned to retrieve the ones she had left just outside the door.

"You went shopping?" I asked. Okay, I had been a bit out of it, but I really didn't remember her leaving and was pretty sure we hadn't discussed a shopping trip.

"Hey, I'm not good at waiting around," Emma said, shrugging. "I brought my cell just in case, but figured we could all use some real food so I bought stuff to make dinner."

"You're my hero," I said, grinning.

"Plus, didn't you say you told the rents you were going apple picking with me today?" she asked. "I grabbed two big bags of organic apples, so you can bring a bunch home with you. They'll never know the difference."

As she talked Emma handed items to Simon and he put them away. They may argue with each other, like non-stop, but those two really worked well together when something needed to get done. I covered my grin with a cough.

"Cool, can I have one now?" I said, realizing that I was starving. When was the last time I ate?

"Sure thing, catch," Emma said, tossing me an apple.

I grabbed a paper towel to wipe it off and caught a look from Simon. The apple may have been organic, but that didn't mean it was bug poo free, just pesticide free. I wiped it off and took a huge bite. *Most delicious apple ever.*

Emma did the same, but apparently wasn't sharing in the apple bliss. Her nose wrinkled up and she spit her bite into a napkin. Looking down at her apple she made a face.

"Gross," she said.

"It's just a worm, kitten," Simon said, looking over her shoulder at the worm.

"Well, he's compost now," Emma said. "I'm not eating this one. Our little friend here had it first."

"That's what you get for buying organic," Simon said, smugly.

"Oh Simon, shut up," Emma said, rolling her eyes.

"You know, I'd eat it if I thought it would keep you away, *doc*," Simon said.

Emma put her hands on her hips and faced Simon, ready for a huge argument I'm sure, but Simon's phone started ringing.

"Saved by the bell," I said. "Or rather, saved by the annoying ring tone." Was that a Spice Girls song? *Really?*

Simon tensed up and began pacing the floor speaking into his phone in a low growl. After a few minutes of pacing he hung up.

"Looks like you won't have to wait after all, love," Simon said.

"Was that the tattoo guy?" I asked, holding my breath.

"That was our man and he agreed to come do your ink tonight," he replied.

Tonight? *Oh my God, was I even ready?* "Okay, but I thought he had this long waiting list or something," I said.

The vampire bats were back to fluttering in my belly and I started to feel sick. I've never been a fan of needles and, though I liked the finished product, the thought of actually getting a tattoo made me dizzy.

"Well kitten, I reminded him who his alpha was and he moved you to the top of the list," Simon said. "I'm curious though, where are you going to get your ink?"

"Yeah Yuki, I was wondering too," Emma said. "You probably don't want it where your parents can see it." Leave it to Emma, always the sensible one.

"I'm getting it where no one will ever see it," I said, grinning.

Simon's eyes gleamed and he leaned in across the counter. "Really?" Simon asked. "Where then?"

"Down boy," Emma muttered.

"My ankle," I said, pleased with myself. "Have either of you ever seen me without boots to my knee? No one ever sees my ankles. Perfect hiding spot."

Simon looked disappointed which made Emma laugh with pure evil glee. While they discussed the spirit-ink man and tattoo art I finished my apple and started unlacing my boots. How bad could an ankle tattoo hurt anyway?

*****

Okay ankle tattoos hurt, a lot. Did you know you have like a gazillion nerve endings there? Yeah neither did I, until a dude stuck a bunch of needles in them. Not my finest moment.

"Ouch," I muttered, again, gritting my teeth.

I felt sweaty and nauseated and was having trouble holding still. So not bringing the tough girl ninja chic vibe to the table today. Spirits of the dead? Crazy werewolf murderers? I can face these paranormal beasties no problem, but come at me with little pointy objects and I go all rubbery. *I guess even Superman has his kryptonite, right?*

We all sat around the kitchen table which was covered in gauze pads and a plastic biohazard bucket where Phil, the spirit-ink man, flicked his used needles. The whole process was evidently fascinating to Emma who asked incessant questions about "blood-borne diseases", "bacteria", and "autoclaves". They were currently in a heated discussion over the differences between varying brands of antibiotic ointments, since apparently some brands would cause the ink to weep from the skin. I tried to tune them out by tracing the biohazard symbol with my eyes, but my attention continued to be drawn to the little metal pots of ink.

Phil was a tall, lanky man with long black hair which he drew back into a pony tail before scrubbing his hands and pulling on surgical gloves. I had managed to settle into the reclining chair that Simon had pulled up to the table and remain calm until I heard the snap of the surgical gloves. My fight or flight response kicked in and I nearly launched myself out of the chair and out the door, but I reigned in my fear...until Phil pulled his tattoo gun out of the case and began attaching the needles. I gulped in air and tried to find my happy place. *Cal is dying and this could save him, so suck it up and deal.* Oh yeah, I was a hero, larger than life.

Simon was entertained by my discomfiture over having a leg and foot exposed. I was so used to wearing thick tights, leggings, and fourteen eye boots to the knee that I felt naked. And everyone was looking at me. Simon's comments about getting a tattoo on "virgin skin" didn't help either. Fortunately Phil distracted Simon with a copy of Inked magazine. Simon seemed interested in the Inked Girls, though that didn't stop the occasional cringe-worthy grin at my bare ankle. *Jerk.*

According to Phil all of his inks were mixed beneath a full moon, something that I imagine involved a great deal of restraint on his part due to the lunar pull on his wolf spirit. He also maintained that all of his inks were vegan. This, of course, made Emma bounce up and down with glee. No animal-based glycerin carrier solutions for these inks. Check. *Got it.* Well, not really, but on with the show folks. In theory, I appreciated the detailed info about Phil's spirit-inks and his sanitary protocols, but in practice I just wanted this whole experience to be over with.

I was trying, really trying, to not puke on anyone, but no promises. The longer they continued talking about blood and needles and ink that would remain forever under my skin the more likely it was that someone was getting splattered. Forever. Tattoos were forever. No take backs. I mean sure, I could have some crazy expensive, and probably painful, plastic surgery or get another tattoo to cover up this one, but since this design was already black it would be difficult to pull off. No, I was probably going to have this forever and a part of me felt a warm, pleasurable satisfaction knowing that. A matching symbol of our love displayed in ink on skin.

Phil continued to explain the ceremonies involved in making his inks as he finished the line work on my tattoo. He talked over the buzzing of the tattoo gun, but his voice seemed hushed and reverent. To Phil the entire process, from mixing ink to the finished tattoo, was a ritual with deep spiritual significance. Calvin and I were binding our spirit animals in a sacred act of love, similar to marriage or matrimony, an eternal union. The vibration and burning sensation of my ankle suddenly seemed far away as I thought about how Cal must have felt when he decided to get his tattoo. He must have been very much in love.

A cool mist hit my skin, interrupting my thoughts, as Phil spritzed something from a spray bottle onto my ankle.

"Soap," Phil said.

Whatever was in the spray it felt good. My eyes were drawn again to the little pots, "caps" Phil had called them, of spirit-ink. They looked relatively normal, but just as my eyes began to drift away I would see a swirling movement within the ink. I also smelled a hint of lavender and honey that seemed to drift in and out with the motion of the ink. Were there actual spirits trapped in the ink? The thought made me feel queasy. *Like I wasn't already.*

I began shifting around in my chair, but stopped when Phil gave me a reproachful glance. I bit my lip, trying to hold myself still. How should I ask him about the movement in the ink? Did anyone else see it, or was it some weird extension of my psychic spirit link? I swallowed hard and cleared my throat.

"So, uh, what does the full moon ceremony do to the ink anyway?" I said.

I tried to sound nonchalant, but my voice came out a bit shaky. Hopefully Phil would just think it was from my squeamishness around needles. I wanted answers, but I didn't want him to know how much I had seen. I picked at my nail polish, which was beginning to look like a UPC symbol of black polish and white nail, and pulled my eyes from the ink caps sitting open on the table. What if there really were spirits of the dead trapped inside? Would I make him stop? Could I walk away from the one thing that may help Cal survive?

Phil didn't look up from his work, but I did notice a sly flick of his eyes toward Simon. *Interesting.* If Phil wouldn't fess up, then I could turn my attention to Simon.

"You should ask Cal that question," Phil said. He was busily shading in the wolf on my ankle and I realized that the time for subtleties was past. If I didn't get answers soon, it would be too late to back out of this tattoo.

"STOP," I said.

The buzzing of the tattoo gun faded away, but Phil looked hesitant. There was something manic in the gleam of his eyes and he hadn't stopped looking at my ankle. Gripping the chair arms, I raised my one booted foot to his chest and shook my head.

111

"Back away Phil," I said. "No way are you sticking any more of that ink under my skin until you explain what's really going on. Spill it."

Phil closed his eyes for a moment and I increased that pressure against his chest, but then he sighed and leaned away, hands raised in the air.

"Okay, maybe I haven't been totally straight with you," Phil said. He looked resigned, perhaps a bit beaten, and I wondered why he would keep something about the ink secret from me. What the heck was in that stuff?

Emma walked up beside me and crossed her arms. "Dude, you are so busted," she said.

Phil looked over at Simon who looked unusually tense. Simon was rubbing his arms and his face had turned ashen. He nodded to Phil then walked quickly to the front door. Hand on the door knob, back still to us, he said, "Tell them everything." Then he was gone.

"What was that all about?" Emma asked.

"That's Simon's story to tell," Phil said.

"That's funny, I could have sworn he just said to tell us everything," I said. My voice was hard and Phil flinched.

"I guess he did at that," Phil said.

*****

I expected there to be lots of skeletons in Simon's closet, but I hadn't counted on a tragic tale of love. Simon just didn't seem the type. Maybe his playboy exterior was just a mask to hide behind so no one would ever get close enough to hurt him again. Just when I thought I knew Simon, I realized that I never really knew him at all.

According to Phil, Simon had fallen for a werewolf girl when they were both still in their teens. The two of them were in love and completely inseparable. When the girl, Meredith, decided to attend the University of Edinburgh right after high school, Simon went with her. They had plans to get married after graduation and underwent the spirit-ink tattoo ceremony before leaving the United States. Simon and Meredith had a bright future together, but it wasn't meant to last.

Simon had more control over his wolf spirit, but Meredith was still young and had to shift into her wolf form a few times a month, especially around the time of the full moon. Since they did everything with each other, they usually shifted together and roamed the nearby rolling hills and fields. One full moon Meredith challenged Simon to a race, and shifting into her wolf form, ran to the North. Simon pursued. Unfortunately they hadn't realized how long and how far they had run. As the sky lightened they entered the area of Perthshire, where over a dozen estates held hunts for live game. At dawn shots rang out and Meredith lay bleeding. Simon grabbed her and managed to drag her away from the hunters, but it was too late. Meredith, Simon's one true love, lay dead.

"That's why this is so difficult for him," Phil said. "The more he has to think about why you are doing this, the harder it is for him. He loved someone enough to get the tattoo once, but Meredith is gone."

"And now Cal is laying there and may not wake up," Emma said. "God, I had no idea."

"I'm sure he didn't want to bring attention to himself," Phil said.

"Okay, I understand why Simon is so upset, but you still haven't answered my question," I said. "What's the deal with the ink? For real this time."

"Everything I have said so far is true," Phil said. "I just left something out." I gave him my scariest glare and he coughed. "It's difficult to explain to outsiders, but the ceremony I performed under the full moon was to call upon our ancestors. Our wolf spirits live on when they enter the next human child, but the human spirits of our pack ancestors leave the human world. When we call upon the spirits during the ceremony, those who wish to help the living return to us and bless the union by giving a tiny part of their spirit."

"There are spirits in the ink, aren't there?" I asked.

"Yes, but just a small amount, like a tiny whisper from a huge symphony," Phil said.

"Yuki, you don't seem surprised," Emma said.

"I repeatedly smelled a hint of lavender and honey when I looked at the ink caps and the ink seemed to be swirling around inside like it was alive," I said. *Or dead.*

"Knowing all of our secrets do you wish to continue?" Phil said. "I want to do what I can to save our alpha, but I won't force you."

I sat back with a sigh. "Go ahead, but I'm doing this for Cal, not for you," I said. I stared up at the ceiling as the tattoo gun began to buzz. Now that I knew the truth I felt grateful that Cal's ancestors were helping us. It was still a bit creepy to have someone's spirit, even just a tiny piece of it, slipped under your skin, but knowing that it was a voluntary thing from benevolent spirits made it something I could accept. I focused on the smell of lavender and honey that drifted faintly past. *Thank you.*

Chapter 18

I had only seen tattoos on other people and in magazines, until today. I turned my ankle side to side looking at the pink inflamed skin. The line work looked raised, like a Braille declaration of love on flesh, but the shading looked a bit dull and my skin was weeping. Perhaps those were the tears of Cal's ancestors crying for his soul. *Don't even go there.*

Phil was fluttering around the room collecting all of his gear. He avoided eye contact, but his gaze would occasionally dart to mine as though involuntarily drawn to me. Phil may have given me the spirit-ink tattoo that I asked for, but he wasn't on my list of favorite people. When he finally packed up and left, I let out a sigh of relief.

"You feeling okay?" Emma asked.

"Better by the second," I said.

"Well enough to help me in the kitchen?" she asked. Emma was pulling an apron over her head and tied her hair up into a knot.

"Sure, so long as you don't mind me in my stocking feet," I said. "There's no way I'm lacing up that boot right now."

"I guess I can let you off the hook with kitchen dress code...this time," Emma said. She started giggling and it was contagious.

"So what are we making?" I asked.

"Stew," she said. Emma tossed carrots, onions and potatoes onto the counter beside the sink. "Wash those while I do the gross stuff."

Gross stuff? I watched, curious, as Emma lifted a heavy pan onto one of the stove burners. Nothing gross there. She slipped a pair of surgical gloves out of her pocket, probably one of Phil's, and snapped them on. Looking embarrassed she opened the fridge and gingerly lifted out a bag of something red. Holding the bag between two fingers she carried it over to the cutting board. Her face was ashen, but she looked determined.

"Is that meat?" I asked.

Emma frowned down at the red substance floating in the bag. "Well it's not tofu," she said.

"Who are you and what did you do with Emma?" I asked. I tried to laugh, but was too much in shock.

"Don't worry," she said. "You and I aren't going to eat it, but Cal needs his strength and Simon...needs his strength too."

Oh. Wow. Emma was doing something nice for Simon? Hell must be enjoying the snow day.

"So what's the plan?" I asked. I started washing vegetables, but was watching her over my shoulder.

"Grab another pan and we'll divide the veggies between the two pots," she said. "I'll add the meat stuff to the soup pot for the guys."

I watched her shrug turn into a shudder, but pretended not to notice. Emma grabbed a knife and set it beside the cutting board. I heard her whispering as she bowed her head, saying a prayer for forgiveness, then she upended the bag of meat onto the counter. With a wet slap the meat hit the cutting board, splashing bloody liquid onto Emma's cheek. She pressed a hand to her stomach and ran outside. I guess I would be the one to cut up the meat.

I was busy slicing the slab of meat into cubes when a ghostly apparition sidled up to my elbow.

"Hey," Emma said. She was always pale, but now she was nearly transparent. I could see veins, blue at her temple, and wondered how much strength it took to come back inside.

116

"I got this," I said, shrugging. "No big." Actually I was trying not to breathe and was pretending that the blood was ketchup, but I tried to act cool about it. "Can you stir the pot?"

"Sure," Emma said, looking relieved.

"So, what happened to evil Nathan?" I asked. "I don't really remember much about last night after Cal got hurt." That was an understatement, since I had gone nearly catatonic. I could see Emma trying to gauge my mood and decide how much to tell me. "Really Emma, I'm cool. I just want to know what happened."

Emma stirred the soup pot more than was necessary. "Well, Simon and Cal had done a number on him," Emma said. "Not that he didn't deserve it. I checked and made sure he was stable enough to be moved, which he was, and Simon called in the cavalry."

"The pack?" I asked.

"Oh yeah, a couple of massive guys showed up," Emma said. "They replaced the rope we had used with real restraints and carried him away. There was a smaller guy with them that seemed to be in charge and Simon said he was the pack shrink."

"So is there like a pack mental hospital or something?" I asked. I tried to picture a ward of werewolves, but the image wouldn't stick.

"More like a pack halfway house," Emma said. "Simon said that the psychiatrist's job is usually providing basic counseling and group therapy when the pack gathers, but he also has a section of his home converted to hold pack members who have become a danger to themselves or others. The doc and his wife take care of them and he monitors their mental statuses. It's ultimately up to Cal, as the pack alpha, but Nathan will probably continue to stay there where he can't hurt anyone again."

"Well, that's a relief," I said. I wasn't sure if I was relieved that Nathan couldn't hurt anyone again or because he wasn't being treated badly. I guess a bit of both.

117

"Did you hear that?" Emma asked, looking toward the door.

"Maybe Simon's back?" I said.

Simon was usually stealthy quiet though. Emma reached for the knife and I grabbed a broom holding the handle out in front of me.

"Well isn't this a fine greeting," Simon said as he stepped inside.

I felt the fear and tension fade from my shoulders and set the broom back against the wall. Emma turned to the soup pots and started stirring furiously, but not before a blush of red crept across her face.

"You better be hungry," she said waving a spoon around.

Simon raised one eyebrow, grinned, and slowly licked his lips. "Of course I'm hungry, love," he said. "I have a legendary appetite."

The blush on Emma's face turned scarlet and I rushed to grab a stack of bowls before someone was stabbed with a kitchen knife or bludgeoned with a soup ladle.

"Simon you want your stew with meat, right?" I asked. I held up a chipped bowl questioningly.

"You girls made venison stew?" he asked, his eyes gleaming.

Venison? I guess that was the meat he had in the fridge. *Great, we just cooked Bambi.* He better enjoy it.

"It was Emma's idea," I said, ladling soup into the bowl and trying not to flinch at the brown chunks.

"You guys had a rough night last night," Emma said, crossing her arms. "You need your strength, so as your doctor I thought we should serve up something more suitable for your wolf palate. Don't get used to it."

I dished out a bowl of stew for myself, the veggie kind, and grabbed the basket of bread from the counter. Juggling the basket and bowl I managed to make it to the table without spilling anything, which was amazing considering I was limping around with one boot on. Emma sank into the chair beside me and Simon was ladling out his second bowl of Bambi stew. For the first time today I felt happy. My ankle burned and Cal was still in a coma, but I felt hopeful that he would wake soon.

Simon set his bowl down with a clank of pottery and grabbed a fistful of bread which he proceeded to shove into his mouth with gusto. *Hello, can you say choking hazard?*

"Don't wolf down your food like that," Emma said. "It's gross."

"Like this," Simon said, with his mouth full. He continued shoving even more food into his mouth.

"Wolf down?" I asked. "I don't think he has a choice."

I started giggling and even Emma burst out laughing. Simon managed to laugh while eating and not even choke. It would have been the best meal ever, if only Cal were awake to join us.

Chapter 19

I tried not to cry as we cleared away dinner dishes. Emma had set out a bowl of stew for Cal, just in case, but he never woke up. My hopeful mood evaporated like the rainbow hued soap bubbles disappearing from the sponge in my hand. Once the dishes were washed and drip drying in the dish rack, we began wordlessly pushing furniture out of the way.

Simon and Emma took their places against the far wall, drums in hand. Reaching down to touch Cal's face I brushed an unruly lock of hair from his forehead and kissed his brow and then his lips. *I'm not giving up on you Calvin Miller.*

Walking to the center of the room, I sucked in a deep lavender and honey scented breath and turned to face Emma and Simon. "Time to dance," I said.

Our dancing and drumming was even more frenzied than before. I could feel Cal's ancestor spirits pulsing beneath my skin in time to our drumming and the racing beat of my heart. Fueled by desperation we ran ourselves ragged, but Cal didn't wake up. There was no sign of improvement at all, not even an eye flutter or a finger twitch. Promising to meet here again tomorrow night, same bat time, same bat channel, Emma and I left the cabin exhausted and discouraged.

The sky was already darkening as we buckled up and Emma started the engine. Squeezing my hand she put the car in reverse and turned to leave. The last thing I saw was Simon's face glowing blood red in the flash of Emma's tail lights. The look I saw in his eyes was heartbreaking, but the river of tears shining red on his cheeks sent a shiver up my spine. Even Simon was giving up hope.

*****

I picked at the remaining flecks of black nail polish and fidgeted on the edge of the passenger seat. When Emma pulled up to my house I flew out the door with a quick goodbye. I had never been so eager to crawl into bed and fall asleep, but I was hoping for a special dream visitation. *I had a date with a ghost.*

Skin tingling I dropped the bag of apples on the hallway table, scrawled a quick note telling my parents to eat up, and ran up the stairs to my room. I closed the door quietly, heart racing, and sank down on the edge of my bed. Unlacing and removing my boots was not fun, my ankle felt swollen and raw, but I changed the dressing on my tattoo and brushed my teeth. Pulling on an old t-shirt of Cal's I had raided from the cabin, I crept under the cold covers and curled up with one of my dung beetle plushies. I tried to quiet my breathing and concentrate on Cal's smiling face. *Come to me.*

Sleep was slow to come, but after midnight I opened my eyes at last in the field of whispering grass. *Cal.* I scrambled to my feet, relieved to see the flowers at my feet blossoming brightly. When the flowers withered and died I would have to race back to my body and away from this shadow world. I needed to find Cal and there wasn't much time.

"Cal?" I said.

My voice seemed to drift on the breeze, sending echoes where sound should not reach. This place had its own rules and I was an intruder. It didn't feel hostile, yet, but I knew better than to stay standing in one place. I started walking forward focusing my thoughts on finding Cal. The direction didn't seem to matter, since the field looked the same no matter which way I turned.

"Hey," Cal said.

His voice came from behind me and I spun to face him as he reached out to pull me into a bear hug. *Wolf hug?*

122

"Oh God Yuki, I missed you," he said, burying his face in my hair.

"Me too," I said. "More than you know."

Cal's lips found mine in a burst of heat that warmed me to my toes. His fingers moved from tenderly caressing my face to slip into my hair, one hand cupping my head as the other ran down my spine to rest at the base of my back. My stomach fluttered and my legs felt weak as his fingers left a trail of electricity down my neck and spine. Our kisses turned hungry and I realized just how afraid I had been that Cal was lost to me forever. *But he's not. He's still here.*

Cal pulled away first as I stood panting in his arms. His blue eyes sparkled with tears, cheeks already damp, and lips red and swollen. I wanted to reach up and pull those lips to my own, but instead I looked more closely at where we touched.

"You're getting better," I said, wonderingly.

Cal looked solid again. He may still be in this place, but he was no longer fading away. The spirit-ink tattoo and my dancing had helped. Nodding yes, Cal slowly turned me to face someone I hadn't seen for too long. His wolf spirit stood a hundred yards away staring steadily at Cal and me. Cal's wolf may not have been at his side, but he was no longer running from him and trying to leap into the light. This was indeed progress and a little sob slipped out before I could stifle it.

"Keep dancing for me Yuki," Cal said, lips brushing my ear. "Dance for me and I will be home soon. I promise."

Chapter 20

October 26th

I woke that morning with tears on my cheeks, but they were tears of joy, not of heartache. Cal was coming back to me. He promised and Cal never makes a promise he can't keep. I jumped out of bed excited and happy as I danced around the room getting ready for school. Nothing could ruin my mood today. *Not even high school.*

I was humming as I added a fringe of safety pins to the bottom of my tank dress. I added a huge silver cross and an artfully ripped cardigan with calavera, stylized Day of the Dead skulls, for buttons. I removed the last of my black nail polish and replaced it with candy apple red. Blowing my nails dry with the hair dryer helped to set the polish and I grabbed my backpack and made it down to the front door just as Emma honked her horn. *Today is a good day.*

I nearly skipped my way to Emma's car, which didn't escape her notice. She raised an eyebrow questioningly as I hopped into the passenger seat.

"You're bouncy today," she said. "What's up?"

"Hot date last night," I said, grinning.

"What?" Emma sputtered. Her eyes bugged out and I couldn't stop laughing.

"A date with Cal," I said. "He came to me in a dream and he looked...better, more solid. I think what we're doing is really helping him."

"More solid, eh?" Emma asked. "Really."

We started giggling as Emma drove toward school. I remained in a good mood, floating down the halls, until a homeroom announcement about the upcoming school House of Horror. I hadn't forgotten the approach of Halloween, but the droning on about upcoming festivities reminded me how little time I had left to prepare for Samhain. I still needed to acquire the fake amulet and plan a stealthy breaking and entering in Salem. *All before twilight October 31st.*

Like that wasn't stress enough, I had an evil surprise waiting for me at lunch. Emma was waiting at our usual table and was nearly bursting to give me the bad news.

"Did you hear about the House of Horror?" Emma asked.

"Seems an appropriate name for the gymnasium," I said.

"So true, but that's not what I meant," Emma said. She slid an orange and black flyer across the table. "Look, it says here to visit the House of Horror to see Wakefield High School's very own resident witch."

I looked closely at the flyer and winced at my scowling face beneath a pointy witch hat. They had even added a large hairy mole to my nose. Painfully aware that we were totally exposed in the open cafeteria I gritted my teeth, fisted my hands, and resisted tearing the flyer into itty bitty black and orange confetti. This had to be the work of the J-team. It had their stink about it. *Jerks.*

"I really can't wait for high school to be over," I said, pushing the flyer away.

"Too true," Emma said. "So anyway, how's your ankle feeling today? You're keeping the dressing clean, right?"

"Heck yeah, I'm even thinking of using it as an excuse to get out of gym class tomorrow," I said.

"Scandalous," Emma said eyes wide.

"That's me," I said, grinning. "The witchy pooh with a freaky tattoo."

I snatched one of Emma's rice crackers and grimaced. It tasted fishy. Since Emma didn't eat fish, I figured the little green bits must be seaweed. *Gross.*

"Karma baby," Emma said. "That's what you get for stealing my lunch."

With a wink Emma slowly ate another rice cracker. I rolled my eyes and was about to go in search of something vaguely edible, but pushing up from the table I saw Gordy walking our way. He looked...determined. *Crap.*

"Don't look now, but here comes Gordy at six o'clock," I said. "Quick question. The Clash, what's your answer?" *Should I stay or should I go now?*

Emma choked on her last cracker. "So not ready for this, but...you go girl," she said. She was trying to smile, but it didn't reach her eyes.

"I'll be right over there," I said, glancing at the nearby trash cans.

I nodded to Gordy as I passed by, but he didn't even see me. His eyes were locked on Emma and when he came to stand across the table from her I could see the tension in his hunched shoulders. *Not good.*

I knew Gordy had fallen hard, but when Emma said she was going to break up with him I agreed that it was for the best. They had only been dating for a few weeks and already an ocean of secrets existed between them. Emma was right to break things off before he got hurt, more than he already was, but it was hard to remember all of that seeing the look on Gordy's face. The pain etched there ran deep and his eyes were full of raw emotion.

"So what's so wrong with me?" Gordy asked. "Was it something I did? Something I didn't do? I really like you Emma."

"You're great, really great," Emma said. "It's not you Gordy, it's me. I've got a lot going on right now."

"Yeah, I know," Gordy said. "That's the problem Emma. You never let me in. You're always busy. You're always leaving and...I'm always being left behind." Gordy turned to leave, but Emma reached out for his sleeve.

"I'm sorry," she said. "Can we still be friends?"

Gordy hadn't turned back to face her, so Emma couldn't see the tears beginning to slide down his cheek, but I could.

"I don't know," he said. "Give me some time."

He pulled away from Emma's grasp and, for a moment, I was torn between running after him and going back to our table. I felt like both my friends needed me, but decided Gordy would probably want his space. Guys don't like to cry in front of girls. With one last look at Gordy's retreating back I walked over and sunk into my chair.

"You okay?" I asked.

"Yeah sure, if by okay you mean feeling like a donkey's butt," Emma replied. "Does it always hurt this much to do the right thing?"

Emma looked up from her lap and her eyes looked sad. No frown lines, no tears. If I didn't know her so well I would have thought she was a total ice queen with no emotions. Emma may be the poster child for calm, cool, and collected, but her eyes gave her away. Plus, while Gordy had been speaking, she crumbled one of her crackers into dust. *Emma wasting food? Surely a sign of the apocalypse.*

I shrugged. "I wouldn't know," I said, twisting one of the skull buttons on my cardigan. "I'm new to this whole relationship thing, but my experience has been either really amazingly great or absolutely horribly bad. I don't think there's much of a gray area when it comes to matters of the heart."

"That was very poetic," Emma said, raising one eyebrow.

"You can buy the t-shirt," I said. I tried to keep a straight face, but a tiny giggle slipped out. "I better grab a bag of chips or something before I faint from hunger."

"Dude, I'm wallowing in my post-break up sorrow," Emma said. "Grab me some too."

"Sure," I said. Emma eating greasy chips? The world really was coming to an end.

"Hurry back," Emma said, holding up the House of Horror school flyer. "We have your revenge to plan."
*****

After school Emma and I met back up in the media lab. I typed up the fake advertisement while Emma made a sheet of sticky labels. Later she would affix them to some small juice bottles, but for now she was making sure they looked authentic. Fortunately the labels only had to pass the scrutiny of Jay Freeman and Jared Zempter, the infamous J-team, which shouldn't be too difficult since they both shared a brain. *A nasty, mean spirited, teensy weensy jock brain.*

The final advertising flyer and labels looked amazing.

Dr. Hoppenjumper's Virility Tonic
Become the envy of your peers. Make girls swoon and cheerleaders cheer.
Contains Dr. Hoppenjumper's patented popularity serum.
100% money back guarantee.
Directions: Drink one cup of Dr. Hoppenjumper's Virility Tonic as needed.

"Do you really think this will work?" I asked.

"Are you kidding?" Emma asked. "Of course this will work. There's no way those two will pass up a chance to both steal something from you and find a way to make themselves attractive to the fairer sex. It's the perfect trap."

"So what do we put in the bottles?" I asked. "I don't want to actually harm them you know."

"Hey, I'm not totally evil," she said with a very evil grin. "Don't worry. No spit, roofies, or laxatives."

"You realize those two have probably already done all three to students this year," I said. "Not that I'm condoning it, but they do kind of deserve the same thing."

"Yeah, well I for one don't want to get expelled or arrested," Emma said. "I was thinking something that tastes really, really nasty, but is actually good for them. No real guilt involved. And it's not like we're forcing them to drink it. They're the ones who are going to steal the stuff."

"Oh, no way," I said, grinning. There was only one thing I could think of that tasted nasty enough to scar a person for life and yet was totally good for them. In fact, it even cured headaches. "You're going to fill the bottles with your headache ease tea."

"You know me too well," Emma said, eyes gleaming.

"You are a totally diabolical mastermind," I said.

We high fived and took our flyers and labels from the printer. The J-team had messed with the wrong witch. I almost felt bad for them. *Almost.*

Chapter 21

*A*fter our fun in the media lab, Emma drove us out to Mr. Green Genes for veggie wraps and caffeine. The chips we binged on at lunch had faded and we both ate our wraps in minutes. Neither one of us left a crumb. Even the soggy pickles, the antithesis of crispy goodness, went the way of the dodo. Emma was still sipping her soy latte, but I grabbed another double shot mocha for the road.

I was nearly vibrating in my seat, cherry red fingernails drumming the dash, as we pulled up in front of the cabin. *Okay, maybe I had a little too much caffeine.*

"Time to dance," I said.

"More like, time to face the music," Emma said, sighing. "I am so not in the mood to deal with Simon."

"When are you ever?" I asked, rolling my eyes.

"Let me think," Emma said, pretending to be deep in thought. "Oh yeah, like never."

"You are so mean to that boy," I said, pushing the car door open.

"Yeah well, he deserves it," Emma said. "And he's not exactly a boy..."

"No, I'm not," Simon said. He appeared out of nowhere. Werewolf stealth could be *really* annoying. "I'm positively manly, though it has been said I have a boyish charm."

Simon looked rakish in a dark suit worn over a black t-shirt. *Where had he been off to? Wasn't he supposed to be looking after Cal?*

"What's going on?" I asked, worry creeping into my voice. "Who's with Cal? You better not have left him alone."

131

"Don't worry, kitten," Simon said. "He's in the adept hands of a beautiful woman."

I felt a flash of searing jealousy, but tamped it down.

"Last chance Simon," Emma said. "Who is sitting with Cal? You know he needs someone with him at all times."

"Why should I ruin the surprise?" he said. "Go on in and find out. After you." Simon waved his arm toward the cabin door and Emma reluctantly stepped forward. He turned to me with a self satisfied grin. "Ladies first," he said.

"No thanks," I said, folding my arms. "You are not checking out my butt."

"Well, you're no fun today," Simon said, swaggering forward.

Simon's teasing caused me to be the last to enter the cabin. I fidgeted with the hem of my dress and nearly twisted one of the skull buttons off my cardigan before finally making it inside to face my potential rival. *Who was inside alone with Calvin?*

From behind I could see a woman sitting beside Cal, her long shining hair cascading down to rest on the pillow beside his head. Her hand reached out to stroke his face and I felt a muscle jump as I clenched my jaw and fought back angry tears. *Who did this woman think she was touching Cal that way?*

"Mrs. *Miller*, so good to see you again," Emma said, glancing pointedly in my direction. "Has there been any change in Cal's condition while we were gone?"

Oh, duh, Cal's mom. I felt like such a fool. Of course she would be taking turns to watch over Cal, at least until the full moon when she and her husband would have to leave town. I glared at Simon who flashed me a satisfied grin.

When Mrs. Miller turned away from Emma, I nearly gasped in surprise. Her face was lined with grief, and the worry over Cal's condition seemed to have aged her overnight. She looked down at her hands as she addressed Emma's question.

"Nothing has changed," she said. "Do you...do you think he'll wake up?"

"Absolutely," Emma said.

"Well then, I'll leave him in your hands," Mrs. Miller said, standing up. "Thank you all for your help."

"Would you like me to walk you back to the house?" Simon asked.

Oh, now he gets all gallant?

"No, but thank you Simon," she said. "I could use a bit of fresh air."

I mumbled goodbye, but was already moving toward the bed. Emma reached it first, but after checking Cal's temperature and blood pressure she stepped away to let me sink onto the chair beside him. Emma and Simon moved into the kitchen, giving me a private moment with Cal. Watching the rise and fall of his chest I thought of all the things I wanted to say. Blinking back tears I leaned forward and whispered in his ear, "I love you Cal and I'm not giving up on you." Pulling away I thought I saw the twitch of a smile.

Emma and Simon were both waiting at the kitchen counter, mugs of steaming tea in hand. Simon had shed his suit jacket and padded over to the kettle with bare feet. He came back with a mug of tea that he set down in front of me.

"What's up with the fancy duds?" I asked.

"Pack business," he said, shrugging.

Okay. "Anything important?" I asked, curious.

"Cal's dad had the paperwork drawn up regarding Emma's scholarship, but a certain number of us had to sign off on the final financial agreement," Simon answered. "Cal had already given his okay, but since the tax involved the entire pack he felt there should be a consensus before it could go into practice."

"Wait," Emma said. "Are you saying there's going to be a werewolf tax...because of me?"

"Yes," Simon said. He looked pained to admit Emma's importance to the pack and I was reminded of the dominance struggle between them.

"Wow," I said. "I knew about their promise, but I had no idea how the pack planned on raising the money. I guess I just assumed there was some wealthy werewolf benefactor."

"You read way too many comics," Emma said. She was smiling, but it didn't quite reach her eyes.

So Emma's wigged out too. *At least I'm not the only one.*

"This is just how the pack conducts business," Simon said. "It's nothing to worry about."

But I was worried and I could see that Emma had concerns of her own.

"Simon, I just have one question, and you better answer me honestly," Emma said.

"No reason to lie," he said, spreading his hands palm out in mock surrender.

"What happens to pack members who can't afford to pay?" Emma asked, brow wrinkling. "I don't want people to suffer to pay my tuition."

Simon barked out a laugh, but I couldn't see what was so funny. His answer could have a major impact on Emma's future. It wasn't something to laugh about.

"What's so funny?" I asked. *Son of a dung beetle.* Simon was really starting to get on my nerves.

"Oh you two," Simon said, wiping tears of laughter from his eyes. "You really thought I'd be out busting kneecaps to get the money."

I looked guiltily at the floor. It was *exactly* what I had been thinking. Shooting a quick glance at Emma I could tell it was what she had been worried about as well.

"Did you really think Cal would go along with that?" Simon asked. "Come on, you both know him better than that. We'll tax those who can afford to contribute and the entire pack will benefit by receiving Emma's medical and veterinary services. Cal is all about protecting the rights of his pack members. I've never known an alpha so determined to have a pack democracy."

Emma looked relieved and I sighed and blew steam from my mug. "I wasn't worried about Cal's leadership," I said. "I was concerned about your interpretation of pack law while he's unconscious."

"Not to worry, love," Simon said. "He'll be awake soon enough."

"Speaking of which, you guys ready for some drumming?" I asked. I pulled off my cardigan and tossed it over one of the kitchen chairs.

"Time to wake sleeping beauty," Simon said.

I nodded and strode to the center of the room. "Time to dance," I said.

*****

The room was awash in the smell of lavender and honey. The heady scent filled me with hope as I stomped my booted feet against the cabin floor. My feet matched the pounding rhythm of Emma and Simon's steady drumming and my arms rose up as I soared around the room. The air felt charged with spirit energy, my skin tingling, and the hair on my arms stood at attention.

Sweat soaked my face as I breathed heavily beneath the porcelain mask and I wished again that I owned something less stifling to wear. Today I had come prepared with a few tricks up my sleeve, or rather tucked away in my backpack. With only four days left before Samhain I was worried that the veil may already be thinning and that evil, malevolent spirits may try to interfere with our dance. What could be more fun for a trickster spirit than to prevent the return of a pure spirit to his body?

Oh yeah, I was taking every possible precaution. Simon had raised an eyebrow when I pulled out the geisha mask and tied it on with the affixed black ribbons, but apparently he was saving his comments for later. I added my evil eye pendant and a wristlet of Tibetan bells. Next I grabbed my carved gourds, Legs and Boo, who I held in my hands as I danced. Spider legs flashing out, bells jingling, and ghost gourd swinging as I twirled and spun.

I called Cal's spirit wolf to me and this time was rewarded by the faint smell of wet dog. I continued to dance and reach out to the in-between realm where Cal and his wolf spirit remained trapped. Drawing on the strength of the pack ancestors, their benevolent spirits channeled through my new spirit-ink tattoo, I called again to Cal's wolf spirit. *Come to me. We need you.*

I swayed, shimmied, and leapt into the air. The geisha mask now felt glued to my face with sweat, but I increased my pace with Emma and Simon's frenzied drumming. I focused on the image of Cal's wolf spirit as the room spun around me like a drunken amusement park tilt-a-whirl. Cool air brushed icy tendrils across my fevered skin as the room was filled with spirits of the dead. Lavender and honey spiced air was rapidly mixing with the scented effluvium of our unwanted guests. *Please Cal, I can't hold on much longer.*

As the gorge rose in my throat, I danced with even greater ferocity. I wasn't going to let Cal go without a fight. I was going to get him back even if it meant losing a part of myself. Good thing they're not at full strength. *Yet.*

Fighting against mischievous spirits, I struggled to focus on Cal and his wolf spirit. I sensed that his wolf spirit was close, but I didn't see him and couldn't catch his scent over the plethora of spirit smells that inundated the room. I felt the room slipping away and struggled to stay conscious, to drag oxygen into my lungs and continue to dance.

Over the sound of drumming, bells jingling, feet stomping, and my ragged breathing I heard a moan that sent chills up my spine. *What the heck was that?* What had we called to our cabin? Eyes wide I spun around looking for the source of the frightful moaning and froze, feet rooted to the dusty floor boards, as movement caught my eye. *Oh my God.*

Emma and Simon stopped drumming and the room fell into stunned silence as we all turned to look into the darkened corner. *Cal!* Cal was moaning, moving fitfully on the bed, and flung his arm over his face as though having a bad dream. Trembling with adrenaline and exhaustion I ran to his bedside.

"Cal!" I exclaimed. "Cal, wake up."

As I reached for Cal's hand his eyes fluttered open to reveal the vibrant blue pools I longed to sink into. He looked confused, but the dazed look was quickly replaced by fear. Cal's eyes widened as he gasped, pushing himself against the bed as though trying to distance himself from us. *From me.*

"Who are you?" Cal asked, voice rasping. "What...what do you want?"

Cold tentacles of fear slithered in to wrap themselves around my heart. *How could he not know me?* Had he returned to us...damaged? I felt a tear slide down my sweat soaked face.

"Yuki," Emma said. Her voice sounded far away. "Yuki, it's not what you think."

"Relax kitten," Simon said softly. "Take off the mask. You're confusing the poor boy and scaring yourself."

"Yuki?" Cal asked, sounding confused.

Oh. Right. In my excitement I had forgotten about the geisha mask I was wearing. I pulled off the mask and set it on the bed. Cal's eyes lit up in wonder as he reached up to cup my face in his hand.

"Is it really you?" Cal asked. "Am I still dreaming?"

"It's me," I said.

I leaned into his hand and his thumb brushed my lips filling me with need. I suddenly had to be closer to him and moved in for a kiss. Cal pushed up to meet me halfway and our lips met, first gently then with the hunger of our recent separation.

"God, I missed you," Cal said, pulling away to look into my eyes.

"I missed you more," I said, grinning.

"Not possible," Cal said, his words brushing our lips together.

Feeling tears roll down my cheeks, I pulled him closer and tasted the salt of tears and sweat mixing with our kiss.

"Ahem," Simon said, interrupting.

I moved apart from Cal reluctantly, but held onto his hand as I shifted to the chair beside the bed.

"Our esteemed doctor thought you might be hungry for something other than kisses after your long nap," Simon said, gesturing to Emma.

Emma stood, blushing furiously, holding a steaming bowl of venison stew. "You need to build your strength, but eat slowly," Emma said. "You've been unconscious for three days. If you eat too fast, you'll be sick."

Cal pushed himself into a sitting position without help, but he sank heavily against the pillows and his hand shook as he reached out to take the bowl from Emma.

"Thanks," Cal said. "I'm starving."

I watched Cal, fascinated with his every movement. Just moments ago he had lain here unconscious, on the brink of death. *And we brought him back.* My heart swelled at the thought, but before I could jump up and give my friends the hugs they deserved I felt someone wrapping a blanket around me.

"You were shivering," Simon said simply.

I nodded my head in reply, suddenly too overwhelmed with emotion to say thank you. I pulled the blanket more tightly over my bare arms and leaned back against the chair. I closed my eyes as the tears streamed down my face with pure unadulterated joy. Cal was back. He was safe, healthy, and awake. My friends had helped make that happen and I wouldn't forget it. I held on to the warm glow in my chest for a moment longer and allowed myself to be the happiest girl in the world. The storm may be coming, but I wouldn't have to face it alone. At the end of the day that was all that mattered.

*****

It was amazing how much had happened since the incident in the cave. Cal had been unconscious for three days and, as alpha, needed to be brought up to speed on recent events.

"So this guy Nathan, who killed Gavin and hunted werewolves, hated us because of his own fear and self loathing?" Cal asked.

We had suspected that the werewolf killer was one of the Old Blood, but it still came as a shock to Cal. I think deep down it would have been easier to deal with if the murderer was a confused human with no knowledge of true werewolves. Though in Nathan's defense, nobody had been kind enough to inform him about werewolves, not even his own mother. Everything he knew was gleaned from his own painful experience which became tainted by encroaching madness. Nathan may have been a twisted killer determined to hunt down and murder werewolves, but he was also a victim.

"No one was there to explain to him what was happening to him when his spirit wolf awakened," I said. "It must have been terrifying."

Simon shrugged, but then he would have a different perspective. He was the one pack member who was born fully aware of his wolf spirit. Of all the werewolves, he was the one least likely to relate to what Nathan had gone through.

"What kind of parent abandons their child and doesn't even warn them about the wolf dormant in their blood?" Cal asked.

"A very, very bad parent," Emma answered.

"Why did the pack let this happen?" I asked. "Wouldn't the old alpha have known about a single mom just up and leaving her teenage son? I mean, I know the pack is really large, but someone must be responsible for keeping tabs on members, right?"

"No," Simon said, looking thoughtful. "No, we didn't have someone like Cal, someone born to be our alpha, when this happened. Whoever was powerful enough could take the position as our interim pack leader until a true alpha had reached the age of maturity, but that meant a lot of fighting and power plays within the pack. We haven't had stable leadership for years. That's why Cal is so important to us."

"I noticed when we were trying to get the word out to the pack about a potential killer that we didn't have any kind of central database for members," Cal said. "I had some information, but there were many people we couldn't reach."

Simon nodded. "It's true," he said. "In the past we were all so worried about remaining hidden and protecting our secret that we never kept accurate records of our members. I think, over time, the active alpha would come to know their pack, but there were no lists of names, nor any way to contact the entire pack in the event of an emergency. Not without going to the alpha for help."

"They used the information for leverage," Emma said. "If the alpha was relied on for that information, then he could maintain his power."

"Yes," Simon said.

"But all that is going to change," I said. Emma and Simon both turned to me with eyebrows raised. "Cal's not like that. I get that there were some power hungry alphas in the past, but Cal would never use his power for himself. He would use his position within the pack to help others."

"Have I mentioned how much I love you?" Cal asked, looking at me. "Yuki's right. Even before the attacks I was trying to make plans for a pack democracy. I have a responsibility to protect the pack and that is exactly what I intend to do."

"No more abandoned teens?" Emma asked.

"Not if I can help it," Cal said. "Simon, let's start working on a central database of pack members."

Simon sighed and rolled his eyes. "No rest for the wicked," he said.

"Emma, I'd like to add our medical records to the database as well," Cal said. "We could use your input."

"Heck yeah," Emma said, eyes lighting up.

Emma was in organizational Heaven, Simon was in slacker Hell, and Cal just glowed. For the first time since taking on the responsibility of pack alpha, the weight of leadership didn't seem so heavy on his shoulders. Being alpha was going to have its challenges, but right now he seemed ready to face his destiny. Cal shined like my very own sun, holding the approaching storm clouds at bay.

Chapter 22

October 27th

I woke from a dream to the sound of thunder roaring overhead. Well, dream is putting it nicely. It was really more of a nightmare, complete with storm clouds of creepy fluttering moths carrying spirits of the dead directly to my doorstep. In my dream though, I lived in a tomb, so my doorstep was this huge, gothic, stone edifice. The last thing I saw as I pushed the tomb doors shut was the icy stare of an angel, carved from marble, glaring at me from atop a nearby mausoleum. As the tomb doors shut with a bang everything went black and I was left alone in the darkness with only the sound of beating wings for company. *Yeah, definitely a nightmare.*

I shook off the left over feeling of horror and slid out of bed. Rain lashed the window and I eyed my warm blankets with regret. Unfortunately I had missed school recently to attend Gavin's funeral and didn't have a good enough reason to crawl back into bed. I guess I would just have to face another day of high school. *I'd rather return to my nightmare crypt.* With a sigh I hurried for the shower hoping any lightning would wait until I was done.

Emerging clean and unzapped I grabbed my favorite red plaid mini skirt, black skull leggings, and baby doll tee. I reached for my black, buckle coat, but the array of straps reminded me of a straightjacket. I decided I wasn't quite secure enough in my sanity to wear that one today. *Maybe after Samhain.* Instead I pulled on a black zip up hoodie and shiny red boots.

Looking in my vanity mirror I scowled and was reminded of the flyer the J-team had distributed around school. *Visit the House of Horror to see Wakefield High School's very own resident witch.* I'm sure Jay and Jared thought they were totally clever with that prank, but I wasn't impressed. Was that the best they could do? Because, seriously, I was getting used to dealing with giant talking dung beetles, werewolf murderers, and stinky spirits of the dead. These things retained a certain fright factor, but the J-team? *Not so much.*

I thought about the bottles of Dr. Hoppenjumper's Virility Tonic Emma was probably filling right now and smiled. The image in the mirror smiled back. A rictus grin leered out from beneath the hooded face. *Spooky.*

I grinned wider, slung my backpack over one shoulder, and took the stairs two at a time. Lifting a huge umbrella from the stand beside the door I flung myself out into the rain to wait for Emma. There is something liberating about splashing around in puddles and Emma later found me doing my best frog impersonation jumping from puddle to puddle.

"Getting in touch with your inner child?" Emma asked, rolling down the driver side window.

"Heck yeah," I answered. "Want to give it a try? We still have time before school." I splashed a booted foot to tempt her out of the car.

"No thanks," Emma said, looking down at her meticulous white dress and vintage cardigan. "White isn't the best color for playing in the rain."

"I'm sure Gordy would disagree," I said, teasing. Wait. Gordy and Emma just broke up. "Oh no, I'm so sorry. I wasn't thinking. That just kind of slipped out."

"It's cool," Emma said. "It's been a crazy few days. You're allowed a momentary lapse of reason."

"Forgive me?" I asked.

"Forgiven," Emma said. "We shall never speak of it again."

"Are you okay though...about the break up thing?" I asked. Things were going so well with Cal that it was nearly impossible to put myself in Emma's shoes, but I knew she must be hurting.

"I'm good," Emma said. "No worries."

"You sure?" I asked. "I realize things have been crazy, but you know I'm always here for you, right?"

"I'm fine," Emma said, rolling her eyes. "Now will you get your drippy self in the car so we can get to school?"

"I guess so," I said. I splashed in one more puddle, with both feet, collapsed my umbrella and scooted into the car. I turned a manic grin on Emma as she backed out of the driveway. "You really should try it. I'll even let you borrow my boots."

"No thanks," Emma said, smiling. "But I know something else that will cheer us up. Take a look in the back seat."

I turned around to see a six pack of Dr. Hoppenjumper's Virility Tonic sitting there innocently; the Holy Grail of payback. I bounced in my seat, for once impatient to get to school. I couldn't wait for gym class. *Was that a winged pig flying in the sky?*

*****

Cal wasn't in school, but that wasn't a surprise. Emma had suggested he stay home and take it easy for a day or two. We both knew that would mean he'd be working obsessively on his project to organize a pack database, but at least he would be away from humans while he continued to recover. The full moon was fast approaching and the combined force of the moon's pull and Cal's weakened physical state could force him to transform against his will. He still had a head injury to heal from, and a nasty headache to go with it, and I was guessing that could greatly interfere with the intense focus he needed to retain control over his wolf spirit. *Better to be safe than sorry.*

Simon would also be at his side which made me surprisingly confident that Cal was in good hands. I still felt odd relying on Simon, but he had proven himself to be reliable, especially where Cal and the pack were concerned. Cal had even confided in me last night that he planned to ask Simon to be his second in command. Vice alpha? Whatever the official title Cal planned to present Simon with the offer today and make a later formal announcement to the pack. That was one ceremony I'd like to see.

I also had business with Simon and needed to talk to him after school. We were now only three days away from Samhain and I didn't have the replacement amulet yet. Simon had offered to secure a replica from one of his underground contacts and pay the hefty fee, something I planned to pay him back over time, but we didn't have much time left. I was hoping that I hadn't placed my chances of surviving Samhain in the wrong hands. Simon may have proven himself reliable, but his underground jeweler was another story. I prayed this wasn't the king of bad ideas.

Our plan to swap out a replica for the original fairy crafted amulet, what the occult shop was calling the Gallows Amulet, had made so much sense at the time. Now that Samhain was only a few days away I was losing my faith in the plan. First things first, worry about acquiring the fake amulet. Worry about the logistics of breaking into a shop owned by practicing witches later. *Preferably way later...like never.*

Cal's empty chair in physics class seemed less ominous today. I managed to walk past it, all the way to my own desk in the back corner, without getting weak in the knees. The past few days had been a waking nightmare, but Cal was awake and recovering. All was right with the world, right up until my teacher walked in and started handing out a surprise quiz. Note to self, next time a scary killer is out hunting werewolves and your boyfriend ends up in a coma, don't slack on your homework. If nothing else, make sure to do the reading.

No teacher is going to accept a supernatural excuse. *A werewolf ate my homework?*

Now why couldn't I date a paranormal guy with mind control powers? I bet vampires could talk their way out of homework and pop quizzes. I tried to picture Cal with pale skin, fangs, a cape, slicked back hair, and glowing red eyes. *No way, totally lame.* I laughed and snorted out my nose, causing a few giggles and an angry frown from my teacher. *Oh and self?* Try not to conjure up silly images of Cal during class. The last thing I need is detention.

*****

I tried to put my gloomy game face on as I headed into gym class. It was hard not to smile while picturing Jay and Jared chugging their just desserts, but if I walked in looking happy they would know something was up. I sat on the bench and set the six pack of Dr. Hoppenjumper's Virility Tonic beside my backpack at my feet. Emma walked in and winked.

Gym class hadn't officially started yet and everyone was used to Emma and me hanging out by the bench. It was where I spent most of my class time. Jay and Jared were horsing around, making fun of our fellow classmates, as usual. When they came closer Emma started talking loud enough for them to hear.

"So, you get your hands on that special tonic?" Emma asked. "I heard it makes girls go crazy."

"Yeah, I can't believe how expensive it was, but if it makes Cal a total stud then it was worth every cent," I said. It was all I could do not to laugh, or roll my eyes, but I kept a straight face.

"It's supposed to make a guy totally irresistible to women, right?" Emma asked.

"That's what they say and it has a money back guarantee," I said. I glanced around pretending to look nervous, and acting like I didn't see Jay and Jared nearly salivating for the tonic. "It was really expensive though, so I need to get it to my locker right after class."

Right then Coach blew his whistle as if on cue. "Today we're running laps inside," he said. "Everyone up."

I hesitated at the bench, trying to look as though I couldn't decide if I should leave my precious tonic unattended.

"Stennings!" Coach yelled. "You've already sat out your quota of classes. If you want to pass this class, which I remind you is a graduation requirement, then I suggest you hit the track."

I groaned, rolling my eyes at Emma who waved in sympathy, and started running. After the first lap Jay and Jared hung back enough to end up behind me, which was totally against jock behavior. I had always been one of the slowest runners in our class. By the second lap I could hear gagging noises and watched as the J-team fled through the locker room doors. I laughed all the way to the finish line. *Who knew gym class could be so much fun?*

*****

"I kind of threw up a little," I said. Emma looked back at me with eyebrow raised. "Just a little, but it was totally worth it. They were gagging so loud it was echoing out from the boy's locker room."

Emma raised her fist and we bumped knuckles. "Gagging," she said, "with a side of humiliation. Now that is what I call success."

"Or one really funky meal," I said. "Speaking of which, any scoop on today's lunch menu?"

"Unless you want meat with a side of meat covered in meat sauce I recommend purchasing a juice from the vending machine," Emma said.

"Just when I thought the day was starting to go my way," I said, and sighed.

I clomped off to the juice machine without enthusiasm. Metallic tasting apple juice, in a can sized for a Barbie doll, was not my idea of lunch. My coins rolled down into the juice beast's belly with a clang, I hit the button for apple, and voila! Lunch was served. I stomped back to our table ready to vent about the injustice of school cafeterias when I saw a fabulous soy pudding sitting next to my bag.

"For me?" I asked, breaking out my manic smile.

Emma rolled her eyes. "Of course for you, but only because you light up like a Christmas tree," she said.

"Well yeah, it's c-h-o-c-o-l-a-t-e," I said.

"It's f-o-o-d," Emma said, smiling. "You get excited about anything you can eat, though I do think chocolate tops your list."

I pictured Cal's warm moist lips and for a moment forgot how to speak. *Well maybe chocolate wasn't at the very top of the list.*

I spooned in creamy chocolate pudding enjoying every bite.

"You're the best," I said.

"All good?" Emma asked.

"All good," I answered. It *was* all good. The school day was nearly over, we pulled off our evil payback scheme, I'd soon be visiting with Cal, and Emma had proven her friendship again with chocolate. Things were very, very good.

Chapter 23

Emma dropped me off at the cabin after school with a promise to return after her shift at the veterinary clinic. She warned that she might run a bit late due to an emergency outpatient visit to a local zoo, but she was obviously excited at the possibility. Emma may have ethical arguments against zoos, but that didn't mean she'd miss a chance to work with rare and exotic animals. Calm, cool Emma was nearly squealing with enthusiasm.

In my rush to see Cal, and get in from the rain, I ran headlong into a wall of leather and chains. Not good. Pulling back I looked up, and up and up, into the scarred face of a giant. I couldn't tell if he was grinning or snarling. The ropes of shiny scar tissue pulled his face in myriad directions, forming Picassoesque geometric shapes, and his eyes were shadowed by the brim of a leather hat.

His leather pants and jacket were getting wet and I remembered how much a leather skirt chafed when it got a teensy bit damp from dancing in a hot club. I made that mistake, once, and vowed never to do it again. This guy was standing there with rivers of rain water running down leather clothing from head to toe. That could not be comfortable.

He was standing beside a shining Harley, one hand resting possessively on the handlebars. Who rides a motorcycle in the rain, in October, in Maine? Maybe he thought it made him look cool, but I couldn't help but wince. There was not enough salve in the world to help the chafing he was going to have later. The thought made me laugh out loud, laughing into the face of a giant.

"You must be one of Simon's friends," he said, offering his hand to shake.

"Yeah," I said. Way to be eloquent Yuki.

"He always did run with some wild ones," he said, winking. He swung one tree trunk leg over his bike and nodded. "Catchya later." He revved the engine and was gone.

Did that just happen? *Weird.* Simon was standing in the cabin doorway as I trudged inside. He was grinning and clapping his hands.

"Very impressive," Simon said.

"What?" I asked. I wasn't in the mood for his games. I was soaking wet, freezing cold, and just wanted a cup of tea and some time with Cal.

"You just laughed in the face of one of the scariest black market couriers I know," Simon said. "Impressive for a wisp of a girl who's only a hundred pounds...soaking wet. I believe you gained his respect."

Cal walked over from the kitchen, steaming mug in hand, scanning my face in concern.

"Great," I said, rolling my eyes. "I now have the scary guy's respect. Just what I always wanted. Whatever shall I ask Santa to bring me for Christmas?"

"It's not something to take lightly," Simon said, looking more serious. "You and Cal are a pair and he is our alpha. There will be times when others will make a play for power within the pack and the ability to look someone meaner and larger in the face and laugh may well save you from a fight." *Oh great, he was serious.* "Plus, the respect of someone three times your size is never something to shrug off."

"Okay thanks I guess, for the advice, but did you say he was a black market courier?" I asked.

"Yes love, I was getting to that," Simon said, grinning. He held up a small black velvet case with a flourish. "Your amulet has arrived."

My amulet.

Cal came to stand beside me, leaning his weight against the wall. "Hey," he said. "You okay?"

"Yeah," I said, feeling breathless. I had missed him so much today knowing he was here and awake, yet out of my reach.

"So you stared down some scary dude and laughed in his face?" Cal asked.

"Yeah," I said, smiling.

"I don't know if I should be worried or salute you," Cal said, smiling.

"I'll settle for a hug," I said.

"That I can do," Cal said, reaching for me and pulling me close.

"Ahem," Simon said, letting out an exaggerated sigh. "Hello. Amulet. Simon saving the day here. Don't I get a hug?"

"No!" Cal and I said in unison. We both started giggling and even Simon laughed low in his throat.

"Well, can we at least do something to celebrate?" Simon asked. "We've been cooped up here for days."

"Sure, what were you guys thinking?" I asked.

"Steak!" Cal and Simon said. They high fived and whooped. *Ugh, boys.*

"Okay, I guess we can go out for steak," I said. "Emma's working a long shift at the veterinary hospital so you both lucked out. There's no way she'd go along with a trip to the steakhouse." I looked back and forth from Cal, who was barely standing on his feet, to Simon. "So who's driving?"

"That would be me," Simon said, jingling Cal's keys.

"You're going to let him drive your truck?" I asked.

"It's his first official job as my second in command," Cal said, smiling.

"No way!" I exclaimed. "Really?"

"See kitten, we have much to celebrate," Simon said, smiling smugly.

Cal put his arm around me and we all hurried, smiling, to the truck. The rain continued to fall in icy sheets, but I didn't feel a single drop.

*****

We returned from our celebration dinner just as Emma drove down the cabin driveway. Simon and Cal retreated to comfy chairs where they rubbed their full bellies in werewolf bliss. I had skimmed the menu for any non-sneeze guard vegetarian food options and settled on the chocolate lover's brownie topped with ice cream and hot fudge. It was that or the baked potato. *I chose well.*

Emma walked in a moment later, tossing her umbrella on the kitchen table. "Where did you guys go?" she asked.

"We went for a celebration dinner," I said, feeling a little guilty. "To a steakhouse."

"We ate steak," Cal said. "Lots and lots of steak."

"There was a veritable steak mountain," Simon said, dreamily. "With rivers of blood and gravy."

"Okay, glad I missed the gagfest," Emma said. "Thanks to Simon's lovely imagery I am now in need of some serious brain bleach. So why the celebration?"

"Simon is my new second in command," Cal said, smiling.

"We were celebrating my promotion and the acquisition of this," Simon said.

He held up the replica amulet he had received from the leather clad giant courier. The amulet shone as the light reflected off its gold surface. It was a perfect copy of the Gallows Amulet now sitting in a glass case in Salem. *Nera's amulet.*

Now we just had to come up with a plan for getting inside the occult shop and swapping out the replica in Simon's hand for the real thing. My stomach felt queasy and I suddenly regretted eating the entire chocolate lover's dessert. I started to fidget and pick at my chipped nail polish, red flakes falling away like dried blood, until Cal slipped his warm hand into mine. He squeezed my

154

hand reassuringly and I immediately felt better. We can
do this. *We just need a plan.*

Emma raised an eyebrow at Simon, but turned to Cal.
"You chose Simon as your second?" she asked.

"He's proven himself and I need someone solid as my
backup," Cal said.

"I've proven my worth, doc," Simon said, gloating.
"What have you done today?"

"Talked to a room full of snakes," Emma said, not
missing a beat. "Funny, they weren't quite as slippery as
you."

"Ouch," Simon said, grasping his chest. "You wound
me deeply."

"Snakes?" I asked. "I thought you were making a run
to the zoo."

"I did," Emma said. "It was the zoo at York's Wild
Kingdom and I took the opportunity to visit their reptile
house."

"Why?" I asked.

Emma had seemed shaken after her past encounters
with talking snakes, but she sought them out on purpose
this time. Maybe her work with Simon had helped her
gain a sense of control over the whole spirit animal thing.

"We have a crazy B&E mission coming up and a spirit
storm on its way," Emma said. "I thought it would be
good to get some inside information. When I heard we'd
be working at the zoo I knew it was my chance to find out
what the snakes had to say."

"Did they have any advice?" Cal asked.

"Kind of," Emma said. "Problem is these spirit guides
seem really fond of riddles."

I groaned from my perch on the arm of Cal's chair.
"Tell me about it," I said.

"Let's hear it," Simon said. "Perhaps our combined
intellect can unravel this great mystery." Leave it to
Simon to actually like riddles.

Emma's voice shifted low and sibilant as she recited:

You seek the Gallows Amulet
Once torn from Nera's hand
Your friend must acquire it
before the spirits haunt the land

Go to the village of witches
enter Cauldron and Noose
access the amulet
before the spirits are let loose

If you wish to save your good friend
go with her to this store
protect her from harm's way
recite this warding at the door

Slither silently and softly
moving small and unseen
curious eyes slide past
minds left untroubled and serene

You seek the Gallows Amulet
Once torn from Nera's hand
Your friend must acquire it
before the spirits haunt the land

"That's all they would say," Emma said, her normal
voice returning. "I just wish they would have elaborated
a bit. I'd feel better knowing that warding was good to go,
but for all I know there's a ritual involved."

"We could do an Internet search on the words they said
to recite," I said. "Maybe it's an old warding spell. If so,
then someone has probably posted it."

"Seems rather straightforward," Simon said, yawning.

"Sorry to bore you," Emma said, rolling her eyes.

"I have a belly full of meat at the end of a productive
day," Simon said. He closed his eyes and was
immediately asleep.

"I want what he's having," Cal said, sleepily.

"As your doctor, I highly recommend it," Emma said. "Yuki, I'll meet you outside."

The door closed behind her with a thump and I leaned in to pull Cal up and out of the chair.

"Okay time for bed," I said. "I'll give you a kiss if you go willingly. That chair can't possibly be comfortable enough to sleep in all night."

"Mmm, comfy," Cal said. "Sleep here."

"Then no goodnight kiss," I said, slyly.

"You drive a hard bargain," Cal said, smiling.

I wasn't strong enough to lift him up, but the promise of a goodnight kiss gave him the extra motivation. Cal stumbled up out of the chair to the bed and crawled under the nest of covers. I bent down and kissed him on the forehead, his eyes already closed.

"Not fair," Cal mumbled.

Smiling wider I teasingly kissed his cheek, nose, and jaw line then let our lips meet in a slow tender kiss.

"Goodnight Cal," I whispered. *I love you.*

Chapter 24

October 28

After a fabulously uninterrupted night's sleep I raced around my room gathering my things for school. Not only was I well rested, but I felt completely energized like the time Cal and I ate an entire bag of chocolate covered espresso beans while waiting to see a passing comet last summer. I was vibrating around the room like a hummingbird when I heard my cell phone chirp. I extricated my phone from the laundry hamper, rescuing it from certain watery death, and flipped it open. Cal had sent me a text message.

"Love you and miss you," the text said.

I messaged him back, fingers flying over the keypad, promising to visit after school. Slipping the phone into my backpack's front pocket I smiled at the memory of Cal's sleepy face. He looked so adorable as I was leaving last night. I couldn't wait for the school day to be over and to be back in his arms. *Planning an amulet heist.* No one ever said my life was boring.

I tried on numerous outfits before settling on my long black and silver panel skirt and black rock star t-shirt with the letters outlined in metal studs. Silver Doc Martens and a handful of thin silver chains slung low on my hips completed the ensemble. I checked my appearance in the mirror. *Not too shabby.*

On impulse I tipped my head upside down and shook like I was at the Headbangers Ball. Standing upright, and slightly dizzy, I added a safety pin to one ear. *Oh yeah, total rock star.*

There wasn't a cloud in the sky, so I left my umbrella on the floor to dry. I pulled on a cropped leather jacket and grabbed my backpack just as Emma pulled into the driveway. *Time to roll.*

I had my first surprise of the day as we walked toward the school main entrance. Jay and Jared were primping and preening, obsessively checking their reflections in the dark, side window panels. They would then strut themselves in front of a group of giggling cheerleaders. I was reminded of the displays male turkeys put on when trying to attract a desirable female. *Two turkeys and a gaggle of clucking cheerleaders. Oh the horror.*

Looking back and forth from the J-team to Emma I tried to stifle a giggle, but the dam broke with a hysterical laugh. Emma looked back at me, eyebrow raised, face and brow twitching.

"Oh my God," I said, gasping. "They still think the virility tonic is for real."

"Of course they do," Emma said, smiling. "They're the J-team; big on muscle not on brains."

I raised my hand and we bumped knuckles. "So how long do you think they'll keep this up?" I asked.

I was blinking my eyes rapidly trying to keep my mascara from running. No matter how hard I tried I just couldn't stop laughing at the Jay and Jared show. *Someone should be taping this.* It was a total YouTube moment.

"We let them steal six bottles," Emma said. "This could last awhile."

"This really is the gift that keeps on giving," I said. I gave up trying to save my makeup and settled in for the show.

*****

I met back up with Emma in the school parking lot after the last bell.

"I want the last hour of my life back," Emma grumbled.

"It's high school," I said. "I want the entire semester back."

160

"But it was horrible," Emma said.

"In what way?" I asked. "Barry Manilow horrible or biology dissections horrible."

"I have to pass health class to graduate, but it's disgusting," Emma whined.

"Ironic," I said. Emma was pre-med, but she couldn't handle health class. *Go figure.*

"But they were doing obscene things with...with a banana!" Emma said. She looked totally scandalized.

"Wait," I said. "Back up. What's this about a banana?"

"The teacher put a condom...on a banana," Emma said. "Do you know how big a deal this is? She totally ruined bananas for me, *forever*. I eat bananas like three times a week. I'm a vegan. This is a travesty!"

"I had that happen once," I said.

"You saw a teacher put a condom on a banana?" Emma asked.

"No!" I said. "My grandmother told me a story of how she was eating a banana and when she got to the last bite a yellow caterpillar wriggled up the center of the piece. Now every time I eat a banana I worry that it's infested with caterpillars."

"Yuki, you're not helping," Emma said. She started to laugh.

"Sorry," I said. "Too much information."

"Way, way, way too much information," Emma said.

"So I take it you don't want to hear about the garbage disposal?" I said, teasingly.

"No!" Emma said, squeezing her eyes shut.

Funny, no one ever wants to hear the rest of that story.

*****

Emma and I went to the cabin after a brief stop at my house for supplies. We spent the evening working with Cal and Simon to formulate our master plan of attack for mission amulet swap.

"I think we should do this Friday night," I said. "I know it's the night before Samhain, but it's also when they're having the annual Salem Witches' Halloween Ball. Everyone in Salem will be there."

"I like it," Emma said. "It's not a school night, so definitely easier to stay out late."

"I wish I could be there," Cal said, squeezing my hand.

"You're sitting this one out," Simon said. "We'll be too close to the full moon and you're still recovering from your injuries."

"It's cool," I said. "And you're only a phone call away."

"I'll try not to shift," Cal said, eyes darkening. "I want to be here for you. I'll have my phone and laptop, so anything you need just call."

"Do I get to be the getaway driver?" Emma asked, positively bouncing in her chair.

"Can you parallel park?" Simon asked.

"Does the earth revolve around the sun?" Emma asked.

"Okay, you're our driver," Simon said.

"I have the perfect hat to wear," Emma said.

"Hat?" I asked.

"You know how in the movies the criminals wear those black knit skullcaps?" Emma asked. "I bought one at the craft fair and have been dying to wear it."

"Okay, so Emma you study the maps and put Cal on speed dial," I said. "If there's a detour or something he can look online for an alternate route."

"Simon, are you coming with me?" I asked.

Originally I had planned to do this myself, but my friends convinced me how impossible that was. We were going to do this together.

"Aye love, I'll be your lookout," Simon said. He looked almost eager to participate. "I'll make sure you remain unseen. If someone attempts to enter the Cauldron and Noose while you're inside, I'll create a diversion."

"A diversion?" I asked. "Like what?" Oh hey, don't go in that shop. There's a burglar inside. *Oh yeah, that would work.*

"I'm a werewolf," Simon said, eyes glinting. "I'll think of something."

"O-k-a-y," Emma said. "How long do we wait for you to shift back?"

"You don't," Simon said. "If things go badly, then you leave as soon as Yuki gets back to the car. You don't look for me, and you don't wait for me."

"But what about you?" I asked. I wasn't comfortable with the idea of leaving friends behind. "We can't just leave you there."

"Yes, kitten, you can," Simon said, shrugging one shoulder. "I have friends in Boston. I can lead interested parties away from the occult shop, shift back, and take the train into Beantown. I'll stay with a guy I know in Southie and call Cal when I'm settled. I can take the train home on Saturday."

Emma ducked her head, face flushing, and swallowed loudly. "But what about your clothes?" she asked. Emma lifted her head up and looked over Simon's shoulder, not quite meeting his gaze. "You can't take the train naked."

"I beg to differ," Simon said. "I don't think anyone would mind."

"Simon!" I said.

"Don't worry," Simon said. "I'll carry my clothes in my mouth. It's awkward, but I've done it before."

"Okay, now that we've settled that issue," Cal said, rolling his eyes. "How are we going to keep your faces off the most wanted list. I'm guessing there are cameras on some of the buildings in town."

"That's the best part," I said. "It's Halloween weekend in Salem. We're going in costume. We can wear masks and blend right in."

"The perfect crime," Emma said.

"The perfect time," I agreed.

Chapter 25

October 30th

*F*riday came too soon. We all stayed up late Wednesday and Thursday night going over our plan, but Friday I spent the entire school day feeling exhausted and uncertain. I would never feel ready no matter how much planning and preparation we had. *Could we really pull this off?*

Emma drove me straight home after school with a promise to meet me there in one hour. I sat on my bed stroking the gold amulet in my hands. Simon had let me take it home last night and I couldn't stop reassuring myself that it was still there. I wet my lips and looked at the clock. Emma was five minutes late. *Emma was never late.*

I climbed off the bed and started pacing the floor. I was glad for the freedom of movement my costume allowed. Originally I had considered wearing a period costume, planning to blend with the large number of reenactment enthusiasts that always grace Salem's historic streets. Unfortunately long bustle skirts are difficult to run in and prone to bumping into things. Not a good idea for a super secret amulet swap. I found myself wishing that I could be as stealthy as a ninja and I thought, why not? Yuki, hot goth assassin, or rather, thief was born.

The only part of me not swaddled in black fabric was the area around my kohl rimmed eyes. It was the perfect costume. I even special ordered a pair of black spiral tabi boots from Ayya. The gray contrast stitching made the spirals stand out against the black leather and in true tabi style there was a space between the big toe and the rest of the foot. *All the better for gripping with.* They were kind of pricey, but totally made of love.

A honk in the driveway announced Emma's arrival and I flew down the stairs and out the door.

"Wow," Emma said, looking me up and down. "You look amazing."

"Thanks," I said. "You look pretty fabulous yourself."

Emma was the getaway driver, so her costume couldn't obstruct her vision. Emma had cleverly solved this problem by using green and gold makeup to give the impression of a mask. She had pulled her hair back tightly and tucked it under a vinyl hood that matched her dark green vinyl body suit. When I saw her yellow slit pupil eyes I felt startled until I realized she was wearing contact lenses. The overall effect was a cross between an Emma sized snake and a Cirque du Soleil performer. *Gorgeous.*

"Did you bring the amulet?" Emma asked.

"Right here," I said, holding it up to the light.

Emma nodded and backed down the driveway. We arrived at the cabin a few minutes later. I fidgeted with my face wrapping and followed Emma inside. Simon was standing by the door, in costume.

"Hey Zorro, where's your hat?" Emma asked.

Simon was wearing a black mask over the upper half of his face and his head was covered in a black silk scarf. The rest of his costume was also black, a silk shirt, top half unbuttoned, and loose fitting pants tucked into soft leather boots. Not a bad outfit for someone trying to be stealthy.

"I, fair maiden, am the Dread Pirate Roberts," Simon said.

"I prefer Zorro," Emma said.

"As you wish," Simon said.

"Hey," Cal said, hip bumping me with a smile. He was wearing a pair of jeans slung low on his hips and an old

Dresden Dolls t-shirt I had given him for his birthday a few years ago.

"Nice shirt," I said, turning to face him.

"Nice disguise," Cal said.

He reached his hands up to the sides of my face and slid the black fabric down under my chin. The cooler air tingled on my skin and then he was leaning in, his warm lips brushing mine in a kiss.

"Promise to be careful," Cal whispered.

"Always am," I said. I pressed into his chest and kissed him deeply. "I'll be back soon."

"I'll be waiting," Cal said. His eyes had gone dark and dreamy and I pulled away before I fell into their depths.

"So," Simon said. "Do we have the amulet?"

"Yes," I said.

"Full tank of gas?" Simon asked.

"Yes," Emma answered.

"Lock picks?" Simon asked.

"Yes," I said, patting a hidden pocket.

"Okay then," Simon said. "Let's go pilfer a magic amulet."

"Swap," I corrected.

"Of course," Simon said. He spread his hands out and tried to look innocent, which only made me worry.

"And just for the record," I said. "We are not stealing anything else. I'm swapping the replica with the real amulet, but that's it."

Simon just strode out the door. Now that's reassuring. *Not.* Emma followed close behind as I gave Cal a tiny wave goodbye.

*****

The ride to Salem was Hell and, fortunately for Simon, I had left my pitchfork at home. On the way to the car he tried to call shotgun and I had to fight him for the front seat. Only Emma's enthusiastic demonstration of me hurling like in The Exorcist convinced him that people with motion sickness get permanent shotgun. Simon dropped sulkily into the back seat, but was soon finding his position advantageous for pestering me. His costume, much to my chagrin, came complete with a pointy rubber cutlass. Simon found it hugely amusing to tickle the back of my neck with it and randomly poke the back of my head. I may have been wrapped in fabric, but the wrappings were thin and so was my patience.

I was so not looking forward to the ride home. *If there was ride home.* I kept picturing us in a lineup getting our mug shots taken; the Dread Pirate Roberts, Snake Woman, and Goth Ninja. I couldn't decide if I should laugh or cry so I settled for biting my lip and stroking the amulet. I was impatient for this night to be over, but that only brought me face to face with Samhain. Not my favorite night of the year. *Not anymore.*

I closed my eyes each time we crossed a bridge, but my fear of bridges was nothing compared to the chill that crept up my spine as we entered the town of Salem. Traffic slowed to a standstill, it was Halloween weekend after all, and I found myself begging Emma to drive faster. She had taken us on an alternate route and we were stopped in front of a dark open expanse. What had at first looked like an empty hillside began to sprout gravestones like crooked teeth as my eyes adjusted to nightfall. *A cemetery.* Of course we would get stuck sitting in front of a cemetery.

Smells started pushing their way into the car and I felt the beginnings of a migraine. Putting my fists to my temples I began rocking back and forth. *Make it stop.*

"Simon?" Emma asked, sounding worried.

"Take the next right," Simon said. "We need to get her away from that cemetery, fast. The spirits trapped here are very old and very angry. With only one night until Samhain the veil is already thinning. Yuki can't take much more of this. Not without the amulet."

Emma pulled the car onto the gravel shoulder and inched past the stopped traffic. At Simon's direction she turned right and then left, again bringing us out onto a road that ran parallel to our original travel route. There was less traffic, though we had to cut through a parking lot to continue in the right direction. *Pesky one way roads.*

"Thanks," I said. My voice quivered and I was still shaking, but the smells drifted away leaving only a dull ache in my skull.

"Sorry," Emma said. "It was my fault. I didn't think to look for old cemeteries on the maps. I just found the most direct route that would take us near Essex street."

"Not your fault," I said. "None of us thought of it either."

"I'm surprised you didn't find a way to wear your arsenal of spirit wards," Simon said.

I pulled on one of the fabric ties and pulled back a layer of my ninja costume. Glinting from every pocket were crosses of every shape and size amidst my other warding charms and beneath that lay my shiny safety pin shirt. I should have been protected.

"It's not working," I said. "The spirits are growing too strong."

"We need to get that amulet," Simon said.

"Good thing we came to the right place," Emma said, smiling.

While we had been talking, Emma had driven us close to the Cauldron and Noose.

"The shop is on a pedestrian road, but if you lean forward you can see part of the sign right over there," Emma said.

"I'll walk with you, love," Simon said, stepping out of the car. "Let's take a look around."

I rubbed the replica amulet between my fingers and secured it in a hidden Velcro sealed pocket.

"I'll be right back," I said trying to smile.

"I'll keep the engine running," Emma said. "Good luck."

Simon and I walked over to Essex Street and blended into the sea of pedestrians. Fortunately people were all walking over to the Hawthorne Hotel where the Salem

Witches' Halloween Ball was being held. I checked my cell for the time.

"The ball started about an hour ago," I said, keeping my voice low. Werewolves had excellent hearing so I knew Simon could hear me over the murmur of voices and rumbling of nearby traffic.

"Looks like some people are arriving fashionably late," Simon said. He swaggered in his pirate costume, but his eyes were deadly serious. "You wait here and do a bit of window shopping. I want to check around the corner."

In a flash of swirling black silk, Simon was gone. I tried not to panic. I walked casually to the shop window of the Cauldron and Noose. It was decorated for Halloween with black bats on strings hanging above an enormous black cauldron. From the top of the window hung lengths of rope tied into the familiar shape of nooses. The display was macabre, but not horrifying. The clown mask staring at me from the nearby costume shop was much creepier.

I tried to look behind the display to the store beyond, but the emergency lighting barely cast a glow over the customer counter on the left and the glass case at the back. I tried to see inside the case, but it was too far away. Glancing around the shop I looked for any movement or other signs of people, but the lights were off, the shop was closed, and everyone was either at the ball or on their way.

A hand gripped my shoulder and I would have screamed if Simon hadn't whispered in my ear.

"Wait five more minutes then begin the incantation at the door," he said. "I'll keep watch. Keep your phone on vibrate. If someone comes near the door I'll either text you to stay out of sight or, if they take out a key to enter the shop, I'll transform in the alcove over there and cause enough of a diversion for you to leave the shop undetected. Remember what I taught you. You'll do fine."

Simon walked away and I continued to window shop. Five painfully long minutes later the street had emptied and I moved closer to the door. I tried to look interested in the flyers taped to the glass while I repeated the incantation Emma's spirit guide had given us.

"Slither silently and softly, moving small and unseen, curious eyes slide past, minds left untroubled and serene," I said.

As I said the first words I dropped a piece of molted snake skin which slid along the ground as though pulled by an invisible hand. I had found a spell with nearly identical wording on the Internet and Emma had helped me accumulate the necessary ritual objects. I sprinkled ash as the spell ended. *That should be it.*

With one last look around, I pulled out my set of lock pick tools and set to work on the lock. I don't know if it was the spell, Simon's assistance, or beginner's luck, but I managed to pick the lock and enter the front door without anyone shouting for the police. I slid into the shop, well, like a ninja, and carefully pulled the door closed behind me. The smell of Nag Champa and sandalwood was intense and for a moment I thought I was facing a smell impression, but then remembered the shop sold incense and essential oils.

Relaxing just a bit, I let my eyes adjust to the room. At the front of the store there were oddments and spell components hanging from wire racks and piled precariously on wooden shelves. Overflowing baskets and bins lined the floor. Careful not to trip, or knock anything over, I made my way to the back of the store. The wall to my left was filled with books on spell crafting, runes, palmistry, and crop circles. A massive display of tarot cards of all sizes stood to my right. The amulet that I had come for sat in the case directly in front of me.

"A Pox Upon All Thieves," read the sign hanging at eye level on the wall behind the glass case. I stifled a shudder and tried to distract myself from the task at hand. I was about to attempt grand theft amulet from an occult shop known to be run by witches. *Son of a dung beetle. How did I get myself into this mess?*

The words were painted in an old-fashioned font and the sign was covered in a false patina of age. My mind latched onto an old memory of my grandmother teaching me the tricks of tole painting. I remember her patiently demonstrating the technique of speckling, layering, and then using tea for the finishing touch.

"See it's nothing," my mind screamed desperately. "It's not even old." Old or not, the sign still filled me with dread.

I was grasping for anything which might distract me, but thoughts of my grandmother only deepened my sense of guilt. I may be rebellious, but I wasn't the kind of girl to steal from anyone. Except now. I felt like I was on a slippery slope to Hell. *Good thing I wore my boots.*

Taking a calming breath, I knelt on the floor in front of the glass case. I tried to ignore the offending sign and not think about angry witches. Pulling the case of lock pick tools once more from my pocket, I set about moving the tumblers the way Simon taught me. I felt reassured knowing he was just outside. This lock was more difficult than the simple lock on the front door, but after a few tense moments I heard the click indicating the lock was open.

I carefully lifted the top of the glass case and held my breath waiting for blaring alarms, armed guards, and killer monkeys. You may wonder why killer monkeys? Watching the Wizard of Oz when I was a toddler scarred me for life. *It's a thing.*

When no alarms wailed, I let out the breath I was holding and lifted the top of the case just enough to reach in and pull the amulet toward me. I slipped the chain of the golden amulet over my head and tucked the necklace under one of the outer layers of black fabric. Okay, half done already.

I grabbed the flap of the pocket holding the replica amulet, but it lifted with a loud ripping sound as the

Velcro tore open. *Son of a dung beetle.* The Velcro was loud enough to wake the dead. Now that was a comforting thought. I froze, hand hovering over the offending pocket, and held my breath waiting for the firing squad. Instead I felt a vibrating from another pocket. Fortunately this pocket wasn't sealed with Velcro. Pulling my phone out, I covered the screen with my body and checked the text message.

"U ok?" Simon asked.

"Y," I answered. Texting was really difficult with gloves on, even the thin ones that allowed me to use Simon's lock picking tools, so I gave up trying to send a more detailed message.

I lifted my hand, once again, to pull the replica from my pocket when a dark shape ran across the floor. Please God, tell me that wasn't a killer monkey. *Please, please, please.*

I glanced around, eyes wide, looking for whomever or whatever was in the room with me. Pulse hammering, I tried not to think of all the nasty things a witch may use to deter thieves from stealing their wares. I nearly threw up when something brushed against my leg. Shaking, I looked down to see two eyes shining back at me. It took me a moment to realize the dark shape was that of a black cat. *Oh.*

I wasn't sure if I should feel relieved or even more frightened. I knew the shop was owned by practicing witches and had read a little about witches using cats as familiars. The fact that it was a black cat, brushing back and forth, crossing my path over and over wasn't making me feel very lucky. *At least it wasn't killer monkeys.*

Trying to ignore the cat, I lifted the top of the glass case and inserted the replica amulet into the original display. I lowered the glass with shaking hands and reached down to pet the cat, now batting something playfully between its paws.

"Nice kitty," I whispered.

I surveyed the room and decided it was time to leave. Stepping away from the cat, I saw the shine of plastic in its paws. What was it playing with? Closer inspection showed a small plastic bag filled with catnip with a fancy paper tag stapled to the top. The cat had only made tiny punctures in the bag so far, but it was getting friskier as it rolled around with the catnip. My inner Emma screamed at me that plastic bags and staples were kitty choking hazards.

"I don't have time for this," I grumbled under my breath.

Reaching down, suddenly very glad for my gloves and thick ninja wrappings, I pulled the bag away from the cat and carefully emptied the catnip into a little pile on the floor.

"There you go kitty," I said.

I tossed the empty bag in the trashcan behind the counter and quickly left the shop. As cool as the occult shop was I said a silent prayer that I would never see the Cauldron and Noose again. Looking up and down the cobblestone pedestrian street, I saw a shadow detach from an alcove across the way. Simon appeared, swaggering in his costume, twirling his cutlass in the air.

"Ready?" Simon asked. "Your coach awaits."

Simon gestured to Emma's car and with a flourish of black silk he was striding ahead of me. Emma, true to her word, had the engine running. I ducked into the front passenger seat, pulled on my seatbelt, and sighed.

"Did you get the amulet?" Emma asked. She had the steering wheel in a white knuckled grip, but her voice was calm.

"Yes, and I saved a kitty," I said.

"You rock," Emma said. She reached over and we bumped fists.

"I hate to interrupt, but the point of a getaway car is to actually drive away from the scene of the crime," Simon said, dryly.

Emma smiled at me one more time then pulled away from the curb. She took us on a different route to leave Salem, avoiding old cemeteries, and we were soon heading north on I-95. Emma was bubbling with questions and Simon was curious about the occult shop's resident cat, but I soon found the sound of the car rushing along the highway lulling me to sleep. I was so tightly wound lately that the need to relax left me melting into a sleepy puddle. I had been so worried about the werewolf killer, about Cal's injuries, and about surviving the spirit storm on Samhain, but now the werewolf killer had been caught, Cal was awake from his coma and steadily recovering, and I had the magic amulet. My eyelids fluttered shut as I drifted asleep.

Chapter 26

October 31st Maine

I was afraid to open my eyes as my brain slowly
sparked awake. Today was Halloween and twilight would
mark the beginning of Samhain, when the spirits of the
dead would walk the land. I reached down and stroked
the amulet hanging from my neck. *It wasn't a dream.*

We really had successfully swapped the replica for the
fairy crafted amulet that protected Nera on Samhain so
many lifetimes ago. I had slept the entire ride back from
Salem to Maine. When we dropped Simon off at the cabin
Cal had come out to say goodnight before Emma drove me
home. *I really hope I hadn't been drooling.*

Emma promised to pick me up later in the day and we
all planned to face the spirit storm together. I wouldn't
have to face my fears alone. *My friends were made of
awesome.*

For the moment though it was Saturday morning and I
was bone tired. I burrowed deeper into my covers, but
froze when I heard tapping at my window. My bedroom
was on the second floor, with no tree limbs nearby, so that
was not normal. *Not at all.*

I cracked open my eyes, hiding in a cocoon of blankets,
and nervously peeked at the window. A black shape was
outlined against a slate gray October sky. Lips trembling,
I called out to whoever was at the window, but my voice
squeaked and rasped like a rusty door hinge.

"Hello?" I said. I swallowed and tried again. "Is
someone there?"

A loud staccato rapping against the window glass caused my heart to beat like a wild animal trying to escape the confines of my rib cage. I put a hand to my chest and remembered Emma telling me that women experienced heart attacks differently than men, but I couldn't remember what the symptoms were. I really hoped I wasn't having a heart attack. "Scared to death my rattling window" would make a super lame epitaph.

Sliding my fingers back to the security of my amulet, I climbed out of bed and onto the floor. I felt exposed crawling in my skelly boyshort pajamas so tried to stay close to the wall and out of sight from the window. Inching my way along the wall, the hair lifted on my arms and I tried to kid myself that the goose bumps were just from the chill air. *Yeah right.* I was scared. What the heck was at my window?

Crouching beside the window I carefully pulled back the dark curtain and saw a close up of the black feathered creature, its head tilted to the side, watching me with one black beady eye. The crow sat there staring at me from its perch. I moved out from my hiding spot to get a better look at the bird. Was it hurt? What was it doing outside my bedroom window?

The crow tapped the glass with its beak and dropped something on the window ledge. Creeping forward I could see the torn wings of a moth. The image framed in my window was eerily similar to the dream I had about the coming spirit horde. With a flutter of wings the crow flew into the gray morning fog and quickly out of sight. The crow was a messenger and his message was clear; the spirit storm was coming.

After that cheery morning wakeup call I needed a long hot shower to wash away my dismal mood. I could feel a headache coming, the dull throb behind my eyes matching the pounding of my heart. Sliding the amulet back over my head I vowed never to take it off again, especially not today.

Glancing in the bathroom mirror a golden glow caught my eye. I turned back to see a shimmer of golden light hovering over my shoulder. I squeezed my eyes shut, hoping it was just a bit of soap in my eye, but when I reopened them the glowing image was still there. *Now that's not freaky or anything.*

Great, Doomsday was nigh upon us and I was seeing things. Could this day get any worse? The golden light shifted closer and the room filled with the pungent smell of vinegar. *Oh yeah, this day could definitely get worse.*

"Mr. Green?" I asked.

I felt a bit foolish addressing the spirit of someone who I knew to have passed over, but the golden light seemed to bob in the air and the vinegar smell grew stronger. That sounded like a yes to me. Okay, I needed to figure out what was going on. For that I needed caffeine. I shrugged a robe on over my tank top and yoga pants and stumbled down the stairs to the kitchen.

"Hey sweetie," mom said.

My parents were sitting at the kitchen table which was currently taken up with an enormous bowl of candy.

"Now *that's* a healthy way to start the day," I said, grinning and gesturing at the bowl.

"Breakfast of champions," Dad said, holding up his coffee mug and a piece of candy.

"You stay out of that," Mom said, slapping his hand. "That's for the trick-or-treaters."

"Think you have enough candy?" I asked teasingly.

That was one huge bowl. It probably held twenty pounds of candy. I hoped my mom didn't expect my dad to lug that thing to the door every time a kid came and rang the doorbell. The poor guy could get a hernia.

"You should bring your friends by for candy later," Mom said. "Your father and I are wearing our costumes again this year."

My dad mouthed "save me" behind her back in mock horror. I think he secretly loved dressing up with my mom and handing out candy to the neighborhood kids, but he claimed every year was "the last year I'm doing this."

"We have a lot of plans, but I'll see what I can do," I said.

I rinsed my mug in the sink and waved as I left the kitchen. The room had been steadily filling with glowing shapes, mostly the golden hue I had seen before, but here and there I saw glimmers of gunmetal gray. I wasn't sure why, but these gave me the creeps. It was getting more and more difficult to pretend they weren't there, so I escaped to my room. The last thing I needed was my parents thinking I was hallucinating. They'd make me stay home for sure and would probably take me to the hospital, a place where people die. That was one stop I definitely didn't want to make on the Samhain crazy train.

My room quickly filled with glowing shapes and a plethora of smells, but my headache had started fading as soon as I put the amulet on after my shower, and though the shimmering images were a new thing they seemed to lack substance. Good. I needed to get dressed and I didn't need any grabby ghosts to get in the way. It was bad enough knowing I'd have an audience. *Ugh.*

Throwing open the closet door, I pulled out a simple black, spaghetti strap, slip dress with gray contrast stitching. Laying the dress out on the bed, I added black and gray striped leggings, fingerless gloves, and a black ribbon choker. Changing was awkward, but I managed to keep my robe on the entire time. When I finally tossed the robe over my vanity chair, I was nearly done. I pulled on tall black boots with buckles up the sides and strapped on a black nylon gun holster to my right thigh completing the costume.

I didn't want to be the damsel in need of saving or a ghoulish creature of the night. Those costume ideas all hit too close to home. No, I was going as a kick butt hunter this year, someone who wasn't afraid to slay some zombies and stake a few vampires before you could say

180

"brains" or "I want to suck your blood." I slid a bubblegum pink squirt gun into the holster and strapped a rubber knife onto my wrist over the fingerless gloves. I pulled my hair up into two messy buns, stray hair sticking out like porcupine quills, and started lining my eyes with liquid eye liner. Checking my reflection in the mirror, I was impressed. *Sweet.*

The weather outside was dreadful, cold gusty wind and icy rain, so I dragged out my full length gray military trench coat. I checked the time on my phone and was discouraged by the still early hour. I didn't want to stay here with a room full of glowing dead people. Biting my lip, I dialed Emma's cell number and hoped she was awake.

"Hey," I said when Emma picked up. She didn't say hello, just sighed when she accepted the call. Not a good sign.

"Unless there are poor, defenseless, fluffy bunnies in need of immediate assistance I am hanging up," Emma grumbled.

"Did I wake you?" I asked.

"I only stopped scrubbing the makeup and body paint off like two hours ago," Emma said. She sighed again and it sounded like she hit her pillow, or threw it across the room. "Bunnies? No? Hanging up now…"

"Wait," I said. "I can be fluffy, and I'm definitely in need of help."

"Give me a half hour," Emma said. "And you're buying me breakfast."

"Deal," I said.

*****

I explained my new glowing friends to Emma on our way to breakfast. We were going to stop at the local diner, I was in the mood for ice cream covered waffles, but the gunmetal gray forms were in greater numbers there, so we went to Mr. Green Genes instead. There was something menacing about the gray shimmering forms. Seeing them in such large numbers sent a shiver up my spine. They seemed focused, and hungry. I wondered if something horribly tragic happened where the diner now stood. Perhaps it was the site of an old battle or forgotten graveyard. I planned to look it up at the library, but not today.

Emma nicknamed the dark spirits "The Grays" which made me think of aliens and X-Files, but it was an apt description. I ordered veggie tofu breakfast burritos, egg for me, not for Emma, and headed to our booth with supersized lattes. It was going to be a long day and an even longer night.

"So are they here?" Emma asked. "The Grays."

"There seems to be at least a few everywhere, but this place is filled mostly with the happy golden spirits," I said. Okay, I didn't really know if the golden spirits were happy, but they seemed pretty chipper compared to the Grays.

"That makes sense," Emma said. "This place has good energy."

"Must be from the coffee," I said, grinning over my cup.

I texted Cal to let him know we'd be coming over to visit soon and Emma and I ate our breakfast in silence. Fortunately for me, I couldn't hear the dead. If I closed my eyes and ignored the strange blend of smells I could almost pretend everything was normal. *Almost.*

The ride to the cabin was anything but normal. I was already surrounded by shimmering apparitions, but as we drove through town more and more spirits came to stand by the road as we drove past. Of course I was the only one who could see them, thanks to my new amulet. The movement of the car, combined with the large number of glowing shapes, created a nausea inducing light show. By the time we reached the cabin I had my head between my knees and Emma was threatening me with certain death if I hurled in her newly detailed car.

"Seriously, Yuki, I just got this car back," Emma said. "I'm all about recycling, but I do not want to see that veggie breakfast burrito again."

"You're not the only one," I moaned.

I sat up straight and opened my eyes afraid of what I might see. *Please, please, please do not be built on an old burial ground.* I needed the cabin, our safe house, to be as spook free as possible. If it was full of Grays we were going to have to come up with an alternate plan, and quick. We only had a few hours until the veil fully thinned and many souls were already crossing over. I hadn't encountered any resident ghosts here in the past, but Samhain left us playing with completely new rules. *Please don't be filled with Grays.*

I straightened in my seat and tried to swallow. The sensation was like parchment rubbing against desert sand. Unholstering my squirt gun, I squeezed the trigger and gulped a mouthful of plastic tasting water.

"Please tell me you didn't just give yourself E. coli," Emma said.

"What?" I asked. "I was thirsty."

"It's your funeral," Emma said with a shrug.

Emma exited the car and I followed. I didn't want to be left behind even for a second. I ran through the rain and into the cabin, hanging my dripping wet trench coat beside the door. When I turned around all eyes were on me.

Simon and Calvin, this close to the full moon, had extremely heightened senses and apparently they didn't need to see my spirit posse to know I hadn't entered the room alone. Cal had his head cocked oddly to the side and Simon was sniffing loudly, scenting the air. With their werewolf senses on overdrive I found myself wishing I had a breath mint. Surrounded by werewolves and spirits of the dead and I worry about dental hygiene. That couldn't possibly be normal.

"Yuki's fan club," Emma said. She indicated the space behind us with her thumb. "They seem to be following her around."

Rather than put them at ease, Emma's comment seemed to make them even more alert.

"It's okay," I said. "The amulet seems to be protecting me so far. There are lots of smell impressions, but they're manageable. No bad headaches and no weird sensations. So far they don't seem able to manifest physically, at least not enough to touch me, but the amulet does have a strange side effect."

"She can see the dead," Emma said.

"Well, kind of," I said. "There isn't a lot of definition, but I see glowing shapes of gold and gray. The spirits that appear as shiny gold seem to be good or neutral, but there are some gray spirits out there that seem evil. I don't know why or how I know, but my gut tells me they are something we should avoid. I think the Grays are the ones that used to come and harm people in the old stories." *Those stories never ended well.*

"I don't like it," Simon said. He was still on full alert.

"Maybe this is a good thing," Cal said, moving to my side. "If Yuki can see these spirits, then we know what we're up against."

"You know, when this is all over, being able to see the occasional spirit that comes to you for help could be kind of awesome," Emma said.

I knew she had been deep in thought over breakfast. Apparently she had been thinking further ahead than how to survive the night. Emma was always planning for the future. It was a skill I envied. Lately it was hard to see past the moment.

"It would be nice to always know where spirits are," I said. "Being able to avoid the nasty ones and having a better idea of how to help the lost spirits find their way into the light. Yeah, that could be a very good thing."

Unfortunately, Samhain was bringing more than just a few lost spirits. *A lot more.* Glowing shapes were steadily drifting into the room.

"Any ideas on how to keep these spirits away?" I asked. "I know they're not actually doing any harm, yet, but it's getting kind of crowded in here."

I was feeling short of breath and although I knew the cause was psychological it didn't ease the tightness in my chest. I rubbed the amulet between my fingers, reassuring myself that it was still there, and moved closer to Cal.

"We have just the thing," Emma said. She pulled out a huge bag and started putting supplies on the kitchen table. "I did some more research and some of these things are bound to help."

"Table salt?" Simon asked. "And is that chalk?"

"We'll sprinkle a line of salt around the room, especially near doors and windows, and the chalk is for marking the walls," Emma said.

"What are we putting on the walls?" Cal asked.

"Warding symbols," Emma said. She held up a book of geometric symbols, some recognizable others bizarre.

"Well, what are we waiting for, love?" Simon said. "Let's get to work."

*****

After hours of warding the cabin, there was nothing left for us to do except sit back and wait. Emma and Simon were amusing themselves with Halloween games while Cal and I cuddled on the couch. I watched as Emma filled a huge wash tub with water and apples. Simon dangled a blindfold in front of her teasingly.

"Are you guys seriously going to bob for apples?" I asked.

"A chance to get the ice queen into a blindfold?" Simon asked. "I wouldn't miss this for the world."

Emma rolled her eyes. "Do you always have to be such a pig?" she asked.

Emma was smiling though, and I was glad they had found a way to busy themselves and have fun at the same time. Waiting patiently was not either of their strong suits.

The next hour was spent laughing at Emma and Simon trying to dunk for apples and managing to get water all over the cabin. Simon managed to get two at once and

Emma squealed as he chased her around the room with his gross achievement.

Finally though, the room became too crowded for laughter. The smells were getting stronger and the air shimmered with spirits of the dead. I burrowed closer to Cal who stroked my hair and murmured, over and over, that everything would be alright. I closed my eyes and tried to block out the raging storm.

One time, when Cal shifted to pull a blanket over me, I made the mistake of opening my eyes. A spirit was only inches away from my face. I bit the inside of my mouth, trying not to scream. The room was filling with spirits, the Grays coming in larger numbers than before, and some were hanging halfway through the ceiling as though peeking in from the roof. Though I could not see their eyes I still felt them looking at me. Cal tightened his arm around me, feeling my unease, and I let him pull me closer. Closing my eyes, I focused on the beating of Cal's heart and the warmth of his chest. All that was left now was to wait here in Cal's arms and hope to survive to face the dawn.

Chapter 27

November 1st

$\mathcal{T}$oday was the annual Day of the Dead. It sounded ominous and I, admittedly, had been harboring a suspicion that today could be just as difficult as last night. *Samhain.* I awoke to a cabin empty of spirits, filled only with the love and support of my friends. I had made it through Samhain without a scratch and with my sanity intact. It was a good day, even if there was the potential for facing down another horde of angry spirits. Nothing was going to shatter my moment of happiness. *Hear that Grays? Bring it.*

"Hey, sleepyhead," Cal whispered.

"Hey," I said.

Cal had stayed with me all night, holding me close and making me feel safe. I appreciated that more than he could ever know.

"The creature stirs," Simon quipped. The long night hadn't bothered him a bit. I wondered if he and Emma had played games all night while I slept.

"Leave her alone," Emma said. "How are you feeling?" She was looking at me intently, doing a full medical analysis I suppose.

"Still sane," I said, grinning. "Well, as sane as I ever am."

Emma reached over and we bumped knuckles. "Good, because we need to stop by your house," she said. She obviously saw my reluctance to go anywhere. "If we don't, your parents will freak."

"She's right," Cal said. "You need to go home and make an appearance, but we'll be right there with you. Simon and I can stay in the car."

"Plus, today's Sunday so your folks won't mind if we steal you away again after your shower," Emma said. "Just make an appearance and then tell them you need to help us clean up the haunted house."

"Ah, that's a good one," Simon said.

"So they'll think I'm helping out cleaning up the haunted house at school, but I'll actually be scrubbing chalk wards off the walls of the cabin?" I asked. They all nodded. "Sounds like a plan to me."

I was glad I didn't have to spend the day alone. I still didn't know what to expect. Nothing in my wildest dreams prepared me for what I saw as we drove through town.

"Stop the car," I said.

I could barely wait for Emma to bring the car to a stop before I jumped out onto the sidewalk. Simon, Emma, and Cal followed me looking worried.

"Yuki, what is it?" Cal asked. He reached for my hand and squeezed. "What do you see?"

What I saw was amazing. I remembered reading about the Day of the Dead and how many people celebrate the day by honoring those they had lost. Flowers are left on graves and an extra place setting was often set at the table for the person in their lives who was no longer there.

As I stood on the sidewalk, I could see a glowing golden shape sit down at the table, at the place left for him or her, with its loving family. Tears started streaming down my face as I saw family after family surrounded by the golden shapes of those they had lost.

"The spirits are with their families," I said. "It's beautiful." There were no Grays anywhere to be seen. "I think today is for the good spirits. The Grays had their night of mischief and now the others are having a chance to say goodbye."

As I watched, the golden shapes shimmered and drifted out onto the streets. Somehow I knew that they were getting ready to depart, leaving their loved ones for another year. Then, all as one, they lifted into the air.

My heart swelled in my chest as I looked on in wonder. Standing here, watching the aurora borealis of spirits shimmering on the horizon, I was happy to be surrounded by my friends and by Cal's arms. I knew that today couldn't last. Tomorrow Cal would have to leave for Wolf Camp with his parents and Simon, where they would spend the days around the full moon in seclusion, but he would come back to me. He would always come back to me. This I knew with all my heart. We were more than soul mates. Cal and I were best friends and we had already stood together against murderers and hungry spirits. Our love would last forever, no matter what would come to stand in our way.

Turning back to smile at my friends, Simon flashed me a roguish grin and a wink and Emma gave me a thumbs up. No matter how bad things may get, or what the universe chose to throw at me in the future, I couldn't be in better company.

"LOVED this book!

She smells the dead is a unique take on paranormal YA
fantasy It tells the tale of Yuki, formally known as
Vanessa who can smell the dead. Well, not 'smell' them
(ick!) but she can smell scent impressions. One day she is
hit with a very pungent vinegar smell and thus, the story
begins.

Yuki is a great main character, she is witty, kind and a
bit sassy. She loves her friends and has a great
relationship with them. Shes into anime, dark clothes and
much to her surprise, her best friend Calvin. Calvin is the
typical YA guy, hes cute and sweet and of course drool
worthy. However, he has a secret, one that Yuki initially
is a bit freaked out about but nothing she can't handle!
Her other best friend is Emma. Emma is the animal
rights activist in the group. A vegan and Calvins
antagonizer she was a fun addition to the story, she's
smart and helps out Yuki and Calvin in a big way later on
in the story. The other characters (Simon, Gordy, etc..) are
well thought out and add charm to the story.

She smells the dead is quirky, funny (Seriously, I giggled
every time I read the words: Bee Oppression) and terrific
for those who want a new spin on your paranormal
stories. While not a very long read, it is entertaining and
the ending leaves you wanting more!"
-Lunamoth, *Far From Reality*

"THIS BOOK IS BRILIANT!!! Okay so I have never seen
a mix of so much going on in one book work so well! You
go from one extreme to the next. Also it is not all
paranormal which is cool, because everyone needs some

great friends and knows what school is like. E.J. wrote such a great book I can't wait for the next one!

You probably have not heard of this book! I hope you have, but if you haven't then you need to read it! I laughed so hard and was in awe of Steven's amazing witty dialogue that I want more now! There is just enough romance that everything pulls together. Stevens left no detail untouched every part of the plot is very intricate and well thought out. You can tell how much she spent writing and editing this because it is so did I say brilliant already? I am not sure how else to describe it! Go out and get this book now! Or go online and order it! You will not be disappointed that you did! Look for Spirit Guide book 2!!"

-Erika, *Moonlight Book Reviews*

"I have just come upon an enchanting new Paranormal Mystery Story written by Dark Poetess, EJ Stevens. She Smells the Dead is just what the Moms and Librarians have been looking for. A New Series of books with enchantment, mystery, love and commitment.

Yuki is our heroine, a high school girl who is affected by the dead. She is "not part of the crowd" At her age, she walks to her own tune, has been called "witch" by her classmates which is exasperated by her looks and dress. To her credit she is very grounded and has a great sense of humor about herself...She has a great friend in Emma, who compliments her in every way. Calvin and Yuki have been friends forever. They share secrets of who they are. Calvin has been told by his family that he is an Alpha wolf, part of his heritage. At a camp they both attended one summer, Calvin finds his WOLF form. Yuki was told she was a DUNG BEETLE which she found unsettling and not humorous. Together in this story, they sift their way through a Ghostly Haunting of Yuki, a need to find out more about their powers and now the young love that is blossoming between them.

Book one of the series is W.O.N.D.E.R.F.U.L. I cannot wait for the sequel....Although this book gives us a great story it ends with the promise of another...Great job Ms Stevens..."
-Gloria Lakritz, *Senior Reviewer for Paranormal Romance Guild*

"She Smells the Dead is the story of Vanessa Stennings, better known as Yuki, as she struggles with and discovers the true weight and meaning of her gift to sense...or smell...the dead. Unlike the glamorous and sensationalized psychics, Yuki's gift can be painful, and the intensity can wear on her. When the sudden, overwhelming smell of vinegar plagues Yuki, she and her friends Calvin, her mystical-loving best friend whose spirit is supposedly a wolf, and Emma, her intensely vegan friend, must unravel the mystery of the spirit before time runs out.

I've been a follower of the author, E.J. Stevens' blog for a long time now, so when she offered a chance to read and review her book, She Smells the Dead, I jumped at the chance. I didn't really know what to expect getting into this book. I thought perhaps it might be a ghost story, or some sort of paranormal story, but it definitely took my assumptions to the next level. Incorporating lore, mystery, wolves, and spirits in an entirely unique way, She Smells the Dead is a refreshing and dark twist on a paranormal story. I thought the beginning of She Smells the Dead was a little slower than I might have hoped, but it established Yuki's background, which definitely helped later in the story. I also had to get used to reading Yuki's thoughts interjected into the narrative, identified as italics. Once I got a grip on that, it became normal to read them, and it didn't feel jarring at all. I really enjoyed, as well, the introduction of characters halfway through, namely Simon, to throw a wrench and a little eye candy to keep the story fresh and alive.

She Smells the Dead is an exciting new take on wolves, spirits, and more. It's a slim book, fast-paced once you get into it, and very easy to read. E.J. Stevens has a unique voice that really sets She Smells the Dead apart from other such books. I give it a strong 4 out 5, and I'd recommend it to all those who love YA, Paranormal, Mystery, and an entertaining read."
-**Melissa,** *I Swim for Oceans*

"I thought the characters were strong and well-developed, and nicely quirky to boot. Even though this is a pretty short book, we see lots of growth for Yuki. Haunted by spirits, she learns to control her ability and seek out the aid of her friends. We see her become stronger as a person. Plus, her gift, clairalience, is such a fresh find in the paranormal genre. How many literary psychics are there that use sense of smell to communicate with the dead? I've only come across clairsentience, claircognizance, clairaudience and clairvoyance and I very much applaud E.J. for branching out."
-**Teresa,** *Read All Over Reviews*

"Yuki is a teenage girl just entering her senior year of high school. Yuki is as far from popular as a green bean is from being ice cream. The jocks in her school call her a witch due to her gothic attire. But Yuki does have a couple great friends! There is Emma, a blonde vegan... that thinks she can smell death by walking into the cafeteria, because of all the meat eating going on there. She is also a pro at making tea with healing properties... They don't taste very good... but man do they work! Emma also is set on freeing bee's from being used for honey. Calvin Miller is Yuki's best friend, he is blonde with sun kissed skin, and strangely always smells like a wet dog! Yuki is also secretly crushing on Calvin, that is until he expresses that he is interested in being more than just friends with Yuki. Oh and there is that small set back that Yuki has.... She can smell the dead! Not disgusting smells like rotting corpses or anything like that but a smell that has left an impression on the ghost. It's that smell that Yuki has to use to solve the mystery that the ghost needs to reveal, because she can't see or talk to the ghost, just smell them.

I absolutely loved every last delicious page of She Smells The Dead! I had to read it in one sitting because I was unable to set it down, I had to know what was going to happen with Yuki's ghost. Better yet I had to know what was going to happen between her and her love interest Calvin! I liked how in one breathe they were just friends but in another Yuki was harboring these feelings towards Calvin. I had no problem believing that Yuki was seventeen, she had normal teenage issues as well as a few that aren't so normal! If you have a chance to pick up a copy of She Smells The Dead, I strongly suggest that you do! It's such a great book. This is also a delightful read with Halloween right around the corner!"
-**Mary**, *Sparkling Reviews*

"If there is in fact a sequel, I'll definitely be picking it up to find out what happens on Samhain!! In the meantime, I think I will actually miss being with these characters! I recommend this for a quick, fun read!"
-**Becky**, *Stories and Sweeties*

"I loved this book it was a wonderful mix of romance and mystery behind everything that Yuki goes though and has to deal with. The story flows wonderfully the way it introduces who Yuki will end up with as well as how she must learn to control her gift, was done perfectly in my opinion. I can't wait for another book because I want to know what the hell happens on Halloween. So EJ Stevens PLEASE KEEP WRITING!!!!!!!"

"This book is part mystery, part romance, part adventure and all the things a person wants!...I seriously can't wait for the next in the series, Spirit Storm!"

"She Smells the Dead provides something new and fresh to the YA realm.

Simple yet thorough writing, a beautiful portrait for a cover, a mysteries that needs solving, the start of a possibly Yuki-epic love story, a rope tying two worlds together, and an added factor of I-Don't-Want-To-Put-This-Book-Down, She Smells the Dead, is a great quick read that left me wanting more."

"Yuki is a unique teenager. She has an annoying habit of smelling dead people. When spirits have unfinished business, they haunt her until she is able to figure out how to help them. Instead of seeing or conversing with the dead, each one has a certain smell that alerts her of their presence. With the help of her friends, Yuki is about to be once fierce ghost whisperer.

First of all, I love the cover. I also loved the storyline. I've read a lot of ghost stories about people being able to interact with the dead and being able to help trapped spirits move on; but none where the dead could be helped without actually seeing or talking to them. It's a different twist and I think that's what made She Smells The Dead so interesting to me. The story was a little slow at first, but once I got a sense of who Yuki was and her ability, I did enjoy the story. I loved her support system. Although Yuki was considered different to most kids at school, she still had Calvin and Emma by her side to share her secret with and to keep her life normal-when she's not being haunted. She Smells The Dead lays the foundation for a great new YA series. E J Stevens did a wonderful job of introducing this series. I am very interested to see what will happen next.

I give She Smells The Dead four flowers of love. If you love ghosts, Goths, and a little bit of YA romance, you will want to check this book out."
-Yvonne, *Diva's Bookcase*

"With its unique take on the paranormal world we all love so much, I recommend it to lovers of all things haunted!...with characters that I loved, and a plot that's as unique as it is interesting!"
-Jenn, *Book Crazy*

"I liked the way the plot worked out. E.J. was able to blend ghosts and wolves and turn it into something very convincing and believable with her writing. I think this was such a fresh idea, a very promising premise that, if worked out effectively would be a really good story. It's enchanting and very entertaining!"
-Kai, *Amaterasu Reads*

"This. Was. Awesome. I've been a fan of E.J.'s poetry for a while because she writes really cool stuff but she's got a knack for Young Adult books!"
-Kris, *The Cajun Book Lady*

"Why I picked it up: Hello, gorgeous. One of my very favorite covers...I just love this picture!

Why I couldn't put it down: I received this one yesterday, started reading it last night and finished it today. After a couple of recent disappointments with books featuring characters I didn't really care for, I am happy to report I enjoyed Yuki and her friends. Yuki came across as a pretty normal, goth-y, teenage girl (well, other than that

whole smelling the dead thing) who likes big boots and anime AND is a vegetarian (veggie characters always make me happy, can't help it =)"
-**Angelique,** *Vampires and Tofu*

"If you thought your high school days were rough...

Yuki's in her senior year and besides dealing with all the inherent pressures of that crazy time of life, she has some unusual and difficult stresses all her own. She doesn't get to see dead people, she has to smell them; her best friend, whom she's beginning to suspect she cares for more deeply than she imagined, has an odd secret that may be related to her psychic power; and her dreams seem to portend an imminent danger.

Author E. J. Stevens' delightfully original She Smells the Dead impressed me from its first pages and I now include it among my favorite novels. Yuki is one of the most likeable heroines a reader has the joy to be introduced to, and I loved hearing her every thought as much as following her story adventure. The author's great character development shines through with the entire cast. Calvin, simultaneously cool and down-to-earth and Emma, passionate vegan and animal advocate, are the best friends we all wish we had. This paranormal romance of blossoming love and great friendships, with laugh-out-loud moments, shares the wonderful "high school can be hell" metaphor and witty dialogue of the TV series, "Buffy the Vampire Slayer," but in a unique story all its own and with the distinctive voice of its talented author. I eagerly await the next book in the Spirit Guide series! Highly recommended."
-**Krisi Keley,** *author of On the Soul of a Vampire*

"What I loved: The characters: Yuki took me the longest to fall in love with, but I was instantly in love with Cal and Emma, her best friends. I think Cal just might be what every young girl should wish for in a guy, well...except for that one little thing. You'll see. (you know I don't do spoilers) Emma is amazing! I love a girl that believes in things that go against the mainstream and trust me Emma walks the walk. Poor Yuki is so overwhelmed at times that she borders on whining occasionally. I have faith that she is going to step it up and be a wonderful heroine. She was very believable as a character with this flaw and that had me loving her as well.

I loved that there is NO love triangle. Now don't get me wrong, I love a good triangle as much as the next girl. However, it's been a bit over done lately and it was refreshing to have a romance that is strong for a change. I loved the story. It definitely has the feel of a first book in a series, lots of set up and getting to know the world that is being created and the rules of that world. It totally worked though.

What I didn't love: The ending!!! Ugh how could you do that to us E.J. Stevens? I can't wait to read the next book! (I guess that's a good thing too.)

Reading this book was fun and at the end frustrating (what a cliff hanger). I would definitely recommend reading She Smells the Dead. I keep telling people that if you liked Kelly Armstrong's The Darkest Powers Series then I think you would like She Smells the Dead. I'm not exactly sure why I think this. For some reason I just thought it had that kind of feel to it. Trust me, coming from me that is a VERY good thing. So grab a copy of She Smells the Dead get comfortable and enjoy. You might not be able to get up till you've finished."
-Shari, *My Neurotic Book Affair*

"E.J. Stevens writes a beautiful paranormal novel with an amazing cover and a story that will stick with you long after your finished reading....Overall I think this book

was well worth the read and I will be reading it again and again. I recommend it to Paranormal lovers, YA, mystery fans. I think young teens could read this with ease of their parents. **5-Roses**"
-Jessica, *Jessica's Vision*

"To begin I really enjoyed the cover art! I like a good book cover and it is one of the first things that attracts me to a book (other than Kelli's recommendations). What also caught my attention was the title, Smell, this was a new catchy paranormal twist that I had not read before. I knew I would enjoy this fun read right from the beginning... I like love and EJ didn't mess around.

The story is based on the new paranormal life of Yuki, a spunky heroine who is experiencing love for the first time and a new-found gift (that delivers terrible smells) all while trying to be a senior. Her two closest friends, Calvin "Cal" and Emma, know about her heightened sense of smell and the dead spirits that follow. Yuki and Cal have a very comfortable friendship that is free of the typical high school stereotype. She is the freak and he is the hippie-jock and it works. It was very fun to read how Yuki just one day realizes that Cal is "hot," it made me giggle and think how blind we are in our teenage years. I also enjoyed the time Cal told Yuki to stay the same, that sends a nice message to youth to remember who you are and love it. Yuki doesn't even think twice to ask Cal to go on her sleuthing adventures... both of them just saddle up and go! The characters in this story are very unique and can easily remind you of different people you might have met or know. The best friend and best friend's boyfriend are an oddity to say the least, from vegan living to anime, what a pair. And of course the mentor that Cal and Yuki are training with, Simon... oh cocky Simon, how I have pictured you in so many ways... his personality is a mixture of Fennick from the Hunger Games series and

Adrian from the Vampire Academy series... need I say more.

The ending is nice and clean and leaves you with a lot of hope for Yuki and Cal but still with a black cloud hanging over their future... will they master their new paranormal powers in time... that remains to be known until the release of Storm Spirit (Spirit Guide #2) set to release Spring 2011... and so the waiting begins!

The Best Thing About This Book:
I loved the sleuthing aspect that goes along with Yuki's gift/curse... This series is like Nancy Drew meets the Winchester Brother's from Supernatural.

Appropriate for a younger audience:
Absolutely, this is a fun quick read for preteens and up."
-Natalie, *I'd So Rather Be Reading*

About the Author

E.J. Stevens is the author of the haunting collection of dark poetry From the Shadows, the chilling collection of paranormal poetry Shadows of Myth and Legend, and the Spirit Guide young adult paranormal mystery series.

E.J. is a graduate of the University of Maine at Farmington with a Bachelor of Arts in Psychology. She has worked a variety of jobs that demonstrate the human condition including schools, psychiatric hospitals and *shudder* shopping malls. E.J. currently resides in a magical forest on the coast of Maine where she finds daily inspiration for her writing.

Visit E.J. at:
http://www.FromTheShadows.info
Learn more about the Spirit Guide Series at the official series website:
http://spiritguideseries.blogspot.com